BÁIRSEACH
THE MIDDING GATE

BÁIRSEACH

The Midding Gate

V B GILBERT

© 2019 VB Gilbert

All rights reserved. No portion of this book may be reproduced in any form without permission from the publisher, except as permitted by U.S. copyright law.

This is a work of fiction. Names, characters, businesses, places, events, locales, and incidents are either the products of the author's imagination or used in a fictitious manner. Any resemblance to actual persons, living or dead, or actual events is purely coincidental.

Cover by Lucidity Design
Original Chapter Art: C.A. Farelli
Editing by: Michelle Hoffman

Created with Vellum

To my Alpha readers

Thank you for loving Onyx

A Witch without powers
A Dragon Master
The dragons call her Báirseach — Dragon Witch

Sage's world is Covens, dragons, and magic. She has two of these three. She's from a loving family, an accepting coven, and she has a job tending dragons. *But magic?* That has always eluded her.

At twenty-seven years old, she has accepted her life as a Mundane. Until Samhain — two accidental bindings and a botched spell placed by her ex-boyfriend change not just her place in the coven, but that of all other Mundanes as well.

Now, she navigates the betrayal of her ex, two new bondmates, and a Warlock full of disdain for all things Mundane. All while hatching the dragon eggs and coming to terms with the separation from her family and the coven.

Sage will be tested through volcanic fire and enchanted ice as she and her company travel from the Midding Gate to Firehaven.
    Who will she be when she returns?
    Will she be accepted?

All she wants is to be normal — a Witch with magic.

GLOSSARY

Báirseach — dragon witch

Midding — v. intr. feeling the tranquil pleasure of being near a gathering but not quite in it — hovering on the perimeter of a campfire, chatting outside a party while others dance inside — feeling blissfully invisible yet still fully included, safe in the knowledge that everyone is together and everyone is okay, with all the thrill of being there without the burden of having to be.

Dia duit —"May God be with you"

Mo Chroí — my heart

Oíche Shamhna Shona Daoibh (EE-hyeh HOW-nuh HUN-uh DEE-iv) — Happy Samhain Eve (to more than one person)

Oíche Shamhna Shona Duit (EE-hyeh HOW-nuh HUN-uh ditch*) — Happy Samhain Eve to one person *alternate gwitch

Samhain is pronounced SOW-in, with the first syllable rhyming with "cow"

Shamna — Samhain eve

Slán go fóill: Pronounced "slawn guh-foyl." — This is a way to say goodbye to someone that translates to "safety for a while" or something like, "hope to see you soon" or "I can't wait to see you again!"

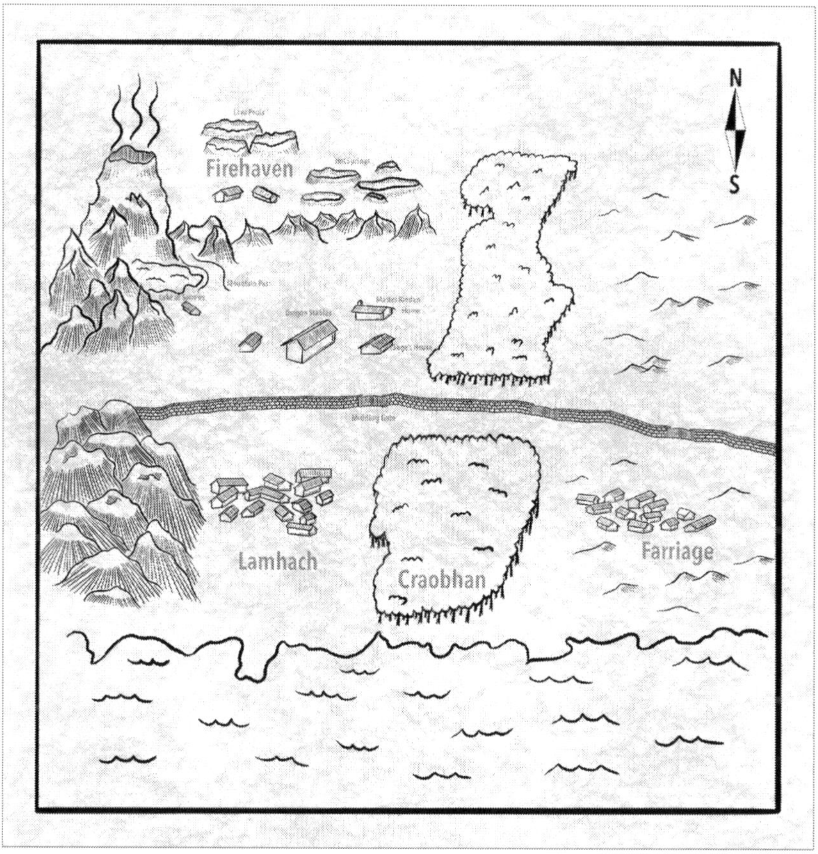
N
S
Firehaven
Lamhach
Craobhan
Farriage

I

Have you ever wished you had magical powers? Perhaps to be invisible, or to halt time, or just to unlock the front door when your hands are full of groceries?

Me, too.

I live in Coven Lámhach. Magic is everywhere. Walking down the street, shopping in the market, in the classrooms at school — everyone doing small and large twists of the wrist, a flick of the finger, a larger forearm sweep — everyone doing a beautiful dance.

A dance I'm invited to, a dance I can participate in, but never quite being in rhythm. A weed amongst the flowers. A duck amongst the swans. That's me, a Mundane amongst the Witches.

I remember the exact moment I realized I didn't have magic.

Mam asked me to clean up some milk I had spilled carrying my cup from the kitchen to the dining room. I spread my hand, then did a curl of my fingers to the right. Just as I'd been taught. Just as I'd been trying to do since before I could remember. Spread. Curl. Spread. Curl.

Spread . . . On the third try, Mam placed a hand around mine and closed my hand inside hers.

We stood there quiet for several long moments, and then Mam gave a little hitch in her breath and in a whisper told me, "Go to the chest in my room. There are several towels in there. Pick the one you like best. Okay?"

I recall peering up at her and wondering why she was standing with her eyes closed and her mouth pinched like she was in pain. She had to urge me on, "Go on, Sage. Quickly now."

At the very bottom of the chest was a little stack of pretty, white towels. They were so fluffy and felt soothing in my hand. When I returned to the spill, Mam knelt beside me and showed me how to sop up the liquid from the floor. How to rinse and wring out the towel. How to clean the floor with a little bit of coconut and lemon oil, then to wipe it with water. She showed me how to wash the towel and let me pick a spot to hang it to dry.

The steps and the motions were soothing for me. It was the first accomplishment I was proud of. It was also the first time I recall *knowing* my mam was crying about me. I knew that it wasn't the result of the fumes from the onions she was dicing.

I was four years old.

Despite the evidence — or lack thereof — of magical skill, I was sent to school to learn all the intricacies of spells and hexes. I passed from class to class, year after year. I received praise for my casting form. High grades for recitation and pronunciation. The only problem was — *my spells never worked.*

I was encouraged to continue my studies, and Mam and Da taught me the Mundane ways of fire-making, cleaning, and . . . living. There was a constant refrain, *"You contribute in other ways to the coven, Sage."*

༄

The light of the day diffuses as a mist rolls in, and I glance at the mountains to the north. Our coven inhabits the pasture land of Lámhach. It encompasses the south side of the peaks, from the sea on the west to the Midding on the east. The members that live beyond the village raise livestock, hunt wild game, or fish.

South of us, is the wooded land of Craobhan. The trees are lush and contain thousands of varieties of plants. The coven there primarily works with plants and excels at building and woodcraft. I visited when I was a child and fell in love with the abodes sheltered within the boughs of the sturdiest oaks.

Farriage, with its hot and dry, desert lands, is furthest from my coven. The members are fire workers — blacksmiths, crafters of fascinating fireworks, and the like. I have never traveled that far south, but I've heard it's beautiful in its own barren way, full of exotic animals.

Lámhach, where I live, is mainly pasture land with hillocks and inclines leading into the mountains. The coven are merchants and craftsmen in textiles and gemstones. There are those with herds of sheep and cattle, which are our main source of wool and food.

The Midding, where I work, is separated from the covens by a stone fence that spans from the sea to the mountains. Each coven has access to this area. It is the entry to the dragon lands.

I like to watch the goings-on in town on my work breaks. I like the colorful wagons when merchants bring their wares for trade. The Enforcers, tasked with upholding justice, come in every now and then for supplies, straight-backed and serious with their blue cloaks.

I watch — from afar. The dragon grounds are just close enough for me. I can enjoy the hustle and bustle of Lámhach, without feeling too crowded.

With a contented sigh, I pull my leather cloak closed, fastening it against the cool breeze that's blowing a light mist across the practice grounds. Leaning against the Midding Gate, I twist the rings on my fingers and watch the newest group of youngsters making river rocks disappear and reappear in the palms of their hands.

Pushing off the rough timber of the gate, I return to my chore of tending the fire.

The stables are at the end of a rough, cobbled path and are much larger than the horses' stables in the village. The walls are stone, and as I approach, the half wall that marks the entry allows me a glimpse of my mentor making preparations for our upcoming trip within the large aisle of the stable.

I load one of my arms with firewood, then grab the long iron pole to move the burnt logs and feed the new wood into the center of the huge furnace. The blaze must stay lit for seven more days. We have seven days before our move to Firehaven and the hatching.

The hatchlings can only emerge within the lava pools of Firehaven. The extreme heat is essential for the wyrms' scales to solidify. Five weeks immersed in the boiling, thick heat of the lava accelerates their growth, and their thick, muscled legs form, aiding in their move to the hot springs. Then there is another three months as each wyrm forms thick leathery wings, and near-impenetrable scales.

If I do my job well — and I am damn good at it — I will return with three full-grown black dragons for the coven. I'm allowed to keep a mating pair until two or three eggs are produced. The pair then returns to the dragon lands after the eggs are laid.

An accord was made ages ago with the creatures. Master Riordan says that the dragons allowed this due to the precarious conditions of the volcano that feeds the lava pools.

Every three years at Midsummer, will be the *Fair and Bewitching* contest. Three trials of combat spells, with one champion winning a dragon.

Then the cycle begins again. We tend to the eggs, and watch over their hatching and growth as dragonlings, the first year. The next two years are spent tending to the dragons, until they reach maturity. If we're lucky, the mating pair will gift us with three eggs before flying to the dragon lands. Then the Fair occurs again, and a champion wins a dragon.

Three years per cycle; this is my fifth since I was twelve and failed my sixth and last attempt at magic. That year I was sent across the Midding Gate to intern with Master Riordan. The coven did not shun me in any way. They gave me a job, a way to contribute.

I shut the furnace, walk around the half wall, and grab a small bale of hay. Making a new dry nest with it, I move the rough matte-black eggs a little closer to the brick warming wall and clean out the muddy wet hay from last week.

This is my life as a Mundane. It's not a bad life working this side of the Midding Gate. I have good friends, parents who are proud of me, a boyfriend, and my dragons.

But, sometimes, I yearn to be normal. I wish for magic.

※

"Sage! Come on, dinner is almost ready," my mam, Ivy, calls from the other side of the stone border. My parents have planned a farewell feast for me. Tonight begins Samhain. Early tomorrow, the Dragon Master and I will be embarking on the two-day journey to the lava pools of Firehaven.

She's caught me as I'm exiting the stables, tired and dirty from a full day's work. I wave a hand in acknowledgment, grab my cloak off the hook, and head to my back door where the wash trough has been set up. Working the fire is hot, sweaty work, and I end up covered in soot and ash by the end of the day.

Grabbing a bucket, I fill it with water then duck behind the brick wall that contains my bathing stall. Quickly stripping, I secure the bucket to a hook and release my black hair from its band. The spring-fed water is cool and refreshing, as I do my best to at least look presentable.

Satisfied with my efforts, I slip into my small cottage via a door on the side of my shower. I've been within the heat of the egg-incubating room all day, but it's almost winter, so I grab a thick, black sweater-dress, socks, and boots to fight off the chill.

Shrugging into my leather cloak, I don't bother going through the Midding Gate to get to my parents' home. Years ago, we made wood steps that allow me to step over the stone border with ease. From there, it's an easy stroll along the cobblestone path through the village to Mam's and Da's bungalow behind their crystal shop.

Mam has her lanterns out to ward off malignant spirits that might be lurking tonight. Harvest has ended, and she's used the last of the pumpkins and carved frightful faces on them.

I pat the one closest to the front door, whispering, "Keep them safe while I'm gone."

With a sharp rap on the heavy wood door, I push through and enter the warmth of my childhood home. Flames flicker in the stone fireplace, casting a buttery yellow light across the overstuffed, floral furniture in the sitting room. A brighter light gleams from the kitchen at the back of the house.

I kick off my boots and place my cloak on a hook before following the tempting smells of fresh-baked bread, roast, and pumpkin pie.

"*Oíche Shamhna Shona Daoibh,*" I greet my parents with a traditional Samhain Eve greeting.

Da rises from his seat at the table, smiling and spreading his arms wide for a hug.

"*Oíche Shamhna Shona Duit*, love." He settles me in the seat beside him as Mam places a bowl of salad on the table and sits across from me.

"*Oíche Shamhna Shona Duit,* Sage. Now, Ciaran can't make dinner, but he'll be by for dessert. He seemed very eager to see you before you left." With a twinkle in her eye, she beams at me. "I think tonight's the night, Sage. Perhaps a ring and a proposal before you leave?"

I sneak a peek at Da, who is frowning and doesn't seem as excited as Mam, before speaking, "Oh, I don't know. He's been . . . distant lately. Ciaran claims it's his advanced potion-making class. That he's been having to do extra tutoring for this group, but he's been different. Curt and almost angry at me."

"Surely, not angry?" Mam serves me a slice of roast then passes the rolls my way. "What would he have to be angry about?"

"You know why, Mam. We've been seeing each other — more off than on — for the last two years, and I think. . . I feel like he only asked me out to try to have an edge on getting a dragon."

I wave my knife in a circle over the butter crock in a learned movement from childhood. If I had even the most basic magic, that would have buttered my roll. But alas, I only look silly and use the knife to scoop a dab of honey butter and spread the creamy goodness over my bread.

"I have no control over who wins the Fair contest or a dragon. I just tend to the eggs, make sure the hatchlings survive, and bring them back when they are almost grown dragons. It's not like I can influence the coven council members in any way."

"Well, then," my da grumps, "perhaps you'll be interested in meeting Padraig's son now?" That's Da's best friend, and since Padraig's wife passed, they have been making plans to move to Lámhach. "He's an Enforcer, you know. He comes through the village often. You used to play together when you were younger. Or you might even be interested in young Murphy. Now there's a good lad."

Setting thoughts of men away, for now, I humor my da, "Perhaps. But you know the requirements of my job. I'm gone from Samhain to the Vernal Equinox."

"Still —" Da is cut off when Mam tosses a roll at him.

"Eoin, leave the girl be. She'll find her mate soon enough."

We finish our meal, conversing about my coming trip, my best friend Rosemary's coming nuptials with Aidan — our blacksmith, and whether or not I'll be able to make a short trip home for the Winter Solstice.

In the back of my mind, though, I wonder about Ciaran. I really hope he's not proposing. His distant behavior these last few months have opened my eyes to the fact that I don't love him. He makes me laugh, and he's good company most of the time. But the fact is, I don't miss him when I'm gone. I am just as content with my life whether or not we interact.

It's not a good thing when you don't miss your boyfriend, is it?

2

I'm washing the last of our dirty dishes when Ciaran arrives. I'm not sure what held him up. He missed dinner, and dessert as well.

His lips twitch up on one side as he observes me washing Mam's china by hand. He thinks it's quaint that I do everything the 'hard way' without any magic. As if I had a choice.

Drying my hands with a towel Mam keeps on hand especially for me, I approach Ciaran. His dark looks are complemented tonight by the grey of his linen shirt and black trousers. He steps close for a kiss, and I offer him my cheek.

Washing dishes always gives me time to think — and I've made a decision. I need to break up with Ciaran. What kind of relationship is it without mutual respect or love?

He barely brushes his lips along the side of my mouth before he hands me a small, silver bag.

"Happy Samhain, darling. This is just a little something for tonight's bonfire."

A long ribbon of the softest black velvet is pooled at the bottom of the bag. Pulling it out, I notice the silver charms on the ends. At first glance, they look like flowing swirls, but on closer inspection, the shapes of dragons emerge.

"Thank you, Ciaran. It's lovely." Carefully, I run it through my hands, enjoying the plush feel of the velvet against my fingertips. "But I can't accept this."

Ciaran's mouth pulls down into a frown at my words. "Whyever not?"

Lifting my eyes to meet Ciaran's, I motion to the parlor. "Let's sit a moment."

Once we arrange ourselves on the loveseat, I place a firm hand on my boyfriend's arm.

"I've thought a lot the last couple of weeks about our relationship. I don't. . . . Ciaran, I don't see it going anywhere lasting." Trying to infuse confidence in my words, I continue, "I feel like you are only with me because I am a dragon tender. Do you even *see* me?

"We always socialize with your friends or attend your functions. If I invite you out with my friends, or even like tonight, with my parents; you are late or miss the outing entirely." Glancing at Ciaran to gauge his reaction, I notice that he's crushing the velvet ribbon in his hand and is staring fixedly at the fire. "I don't mean to hurt you. But I think it's best we break up."

Ciaran takes a deep breath and loosens his hold on the ribbon. Through gritted teeth he speaks, "Sage, I need you in my life. Can we . . . can we take a break instead? There's five weeks until Rosemary's wedding. Let's see each other as friends then revisit this before the wedding. I can't lose you."

While I'm touched Ciaran wants to remain friends, I'm confused about 'seeing' him the next five weeks. "I'm more than willing to be your friend, but Ciaran, I'll be in Firehaven until the Winter Solstice."

"I thought with Rosemary's wedding approaching that you would delay your departure. As her best friend, are you not expected to help her with wedding-type things?"

Delay? Why would I delay my departure?

Biting the corner of my lip, I search for the correct words to say. I generally try to be very even-tempered, but at the moment, I'm appalled that he thinks I could just not go to work for five weeks.

"Ciaran, I can't stay at home for five weeks. I have a job — a duty

— to tend to the hatchlings. Master Riordan is preparing me to take over for him. And this year, Renny will begin his internship."

"Yes, he'll have a new intern. You won't be leaving him in the lurch," Ciaran says as he overrides my next words.

I have to restrain myself from speaking rudely.

"Renny is having a rough time. The first year is the hardest, Ciaran. Learning the trade and also dealing with the fact that he will never have magic — he needs my support."

I play on Ciaran's empathy, even though I know it's a futile effort. He does not *want* to understand nor is he willing to *try* to understand the life of a Mundane.

Ciaran stands and straightens the sharp lines of his trousers before offering me a hand. "If you won't delay, you *will* be back at Winter Solstice. Missing this year will not do, Sage."

"Um . . . I *will try* to be back. Not because you are demanding it, but because I promised Rosemary."

I begin to gather my things for tonight — a bag of caramels, my cloak — and pause in the midst of pulling on my boots.

"What is going on with you, Ciaran? This overbearing behavior is not you."

Some emotion passes behind his eyes too quickly for me to decipher before he bestows a charming grin on me.

"I'll just miss you, darling. The five weeks before you return is a long time for you to be gone. No worries. I thought you were staying home, and I was mistaken."

Ushering me out the front door, he places my hand in the crook of his elbow. "Come. Let's not be late for the festivities."

※

Samhain has always been my favorite time of year. As Ciaran and I approach the practice grounds, I delight in the decorations. Torches line the path and outer perimeter of the field. The trees have fairy lights hanging from their branches, and, of course, the bonfire dominates the central meeting area.

A brisk wind has the flames flickering and jumping. I gather the edges of my cloak close and pop the hood up, greeting friends as we pass food stands and game areas. The children pounce on me when they see my purple bag, threatening hexes and jinxes if I don't give them a treat.

Laughing at their antics, I pretend to be afraid before handing out caramels to each trickster.

It's while I'm kneeling in front of my cousin's youngest girl, Lavender, that I notice Ciaran has continued on without me. I've lost sight of him. Not overly concerned, I continue on my own; I enjoy looking at all the various ways the festival-goers have individualized their traditional black garb.

Some, like me, have a bright-colored bag. A few of the men have worn colorful ties or bright-tone accent pieces. The children all seem to have focused their spot of color on striped socks and colorful shoes.

"Sage! Sage! Over here!" Rosemary's voice rivals the hum of the crowd.

I catch sight of her at her mother's fabric stand. Rushing over, I give her a hug then hold her arms as I admire her off-the-shoulder dress. Her long, brown locks are swept into a bun. Yellow bows give her a pop of brightness against her hair, wrists, and neck.

"You look gorgeous as ever, Rose. Where's that man of yours?"

I stow my cloak under the counter of her booth, and I peek around her shoulder into the stall, looking for Aidan, but only see spools of ribbon and bolts of fabric.

"Aidan and his new partner, Egan, are doing a demonstration at the forge. They'll be here soon. Where's Ciaran?"

She pulls two lengths of thin, purple ribbon then forces me to sit at her stool and expertly gathers my straight, black hair into a high ponytail. With a gentle hand, she weaves the thin ribbon into my hair as she braids it.

With a sigh, I look out into the crowd. Still no Ciaran. "We have decided to take a break. I tried to break up with him — I've told you how he's been acting strange lately. He wants to try as friends. So, I agreed to still come to the festival with him, but I've lost him, as usual. I'm sure he's networking with the other teachers. He hopes to get elected Headmaster next year."

Tying my braid off with a bow, Rosemary gives it a tug. "How do you think it will be as friends?"

Spinning on the stool, I look up at my best friend. "I don't think it will end well. He's stubborn and insistent he needs me in his life. But enough about Ciaran, I came out to enjoy the evening, and I don't want to dwell on him anymore." Standing, I give my best friend a hug, "Someday, I'll find a good man like Aidan. Someone who will respect me, treat me well, and not care that I'm a Mundane. Tonight, however, I just want to dance."

A tinkling of bells starts up. It's the signal that the dancing and the *Spell of Light and Renewal* are beginning.

With broad grins, we secure her stand and run to take our places with the others encircling the bonfire. As we jostle for position, Aidan and a large, raven-haired man end up beside us, and I find myself between the two men.

I strain to see if I can catch a glimpse of Ciaran, since I did come with him, but it's too crowded. Before I can decide if I should walk around to find him, the elders call for everyone to settle down.

Elder Thyme — no really, that's her name — instructs us to pair off. Rosemary, of course, grabs her fiancé, Aidan. The man to my right introduces himself as Aidan's coworker, Egan. He gives me a shy grin and a raised brow.

"Would you do me the honor, Miss Sage?" Expectantly, he holds out one hand towards me.

"I'd be honored, Egan. But I'm Mundane. You realize I might hinder your spell?" I feel it's my duty to warn him. I know the words and the steps, but with no magic, I often dampen a partner's spell casting.

"I'm willing to chance it if you are." He places our arms so that they are intertwined in front of us. Left hand to left hand, right hand to right, forming an infinity symbol across our torsos.

Excited, I bounce on the balls of my feet. I am always humbled that the coven allows me to participate.

Egan chuckles beside me. When I glance up at him, I notice how the flames heighten the amber color of his eyes, making them look like warm sparks. With a squeeze of his hands, he leads me through the steps.

We dip and twirl, never breaking contact as the spell requires.

Harvest is done
And winter comes
The festival fire is burning bright
Chasing off evil with its light

By Goddess grace
We inhabit this place
Giving as much as we receive
All that we do, by her leave

Egan and I twirl faster and faster as the chant continues. Pulse pounding in rhythm to our steps, each turn flashes bright with the fire then dimmer as we turn away. On and on until. . . .

So mote it be!

The fire flares in the Samhain wind, sparks floating up to mix with the twinkling starlight above.

A moment of silence stretches out before it's shattered by laughter and gasping breaths of the coven. Another successful Samhain Eve.

Tingling in my hands reminds me that Egan and I are still connected.

He holds on a beat longer when I move to pull away, then bows deeply to me. "Thank you for the dance, Miss Sage." Moving closer, he tugs on my braid before whispering in my ear. "You aren't without magic. That was the most spellbinding dance I've had in ages."

With those parting words, he disappears into the crowd.

I'm still standing speechless when Ciaran finds me.

"Where have you been? I've been looking all over for you. I had to dance with *Thistle*. You know she's been competing with me for the Headmaster position." He continues to gripe, and it's putting a damper on my joy of the evening.

"No, Ciaran, you walked off and left me — as usual. This is one of many reasons why you and I are not working out." He continues to gripe and tries to put a damper on my joy of the evening. "You will not ruin my good mood. Go on. Go do your networking and socializing. I'm going to enjoy the rest of my night."

I wave my hands at him, shooing him away.

"Sage! What has come over you?" The disapproval rings clear in Ciaran's words, but I ignore him.

Smiling, I wave at Rosemary and turn to join her. As I pass Ciaran, I reply to his question. "A spell. A spell has come over me."

3

I find Rosemary, Aidan, and Egan sitting on hay bales beside the stone wall that marks the border into the dragon grounds. I hurry to join them, only stopping once to grab a bottle of lavender lemonade and a large bag of roasted nuts.

"We meet again, my little spellbinder." Egan offers me the space beside Rosemary before taking a seat behind me on a two-bale-high stack. If I lean back at all, I will be bracketed by his legs.

"Miss Sage, how long have you and Rosemary been friends?" Egan leans forward and peers around my right shoulder to ask his question. His long bangs fall across his forehead as his eyes play hide-and-seek behind the ebony strands.

I fill the cups that Egan conjures with lemonade before answering. "Oh, we were very young. We were neighbors and our parents have side-by-side shops. We played in the garden while they worked. I would trade small crystal shards for some of Rosemary's ribbon trimmings. We were like little crows, hoarding tidbits of castoffs and remnants from the various shops." Glancing at Rosemary, I reminisce, "Do you remember how Murphy used to tease us about our 'treasures'?"

Eagerly, Rosemary nods her head. "Aye, he's a good friend, but he teased us mercilessly as children." Leaning her head on her fiancé's arm she continues. "Aidan, you remember the mosaic on the back of the garden bench? That was Sage's doing. When she was twelve and given the job of dragon intern, she took all our treasures and made that beautiful dragon image for me."

"I didn't want you to forget me while you were at school and I was learning my trade." I passed around the bag of nuts, giggling. "Which was silly, since we still saw each other in the evenings and on the weekends."

Placing my cup on the grass at my seat, I sit back up to find myself within the circle of Egan's arms. He has leaned forward and is resting his elbows on his knees, hands dangling by my upper arms.

I'm not uncomfortable, but I shift sideways in order to meet his gaze as I inquire, "And you, Egan? Where do you hail from? Are you a blacksmith as well? Rosemary told me that you and Aidan were hosting a demonstration at the forge earlier."

"My coven reside in Farraige. Aidan sent word he needed help last month, so here I am. I am a trained blacksmith, but I specialize in metalwork and jewelry making."

I feel a tug on my scalp as he's speaking. Egan has my braid in hand and is deftly unbraiding it.

Startled, I grab at his hands, but I'm too late. The heavy weight of my hair falls on my shoulders. Gathering the ends, I hold them at my left shoulder and stare incredulously at this bold man. "Whyever did you do that?"

"In my coven, only the women wed or widowed wear their hair completely bound. You, Miss Sage, are neither. Turn back around, and I'll make you a loose ponytail, so the wind doesn't knot it." With a gentle grip on my shoulder, Egan turns me, so I am facing the bonfire again.

From the corner of my eye, I can see my best friend giving me *the look*. The one that seems to communicate, '*He likes you, he likes you.*' It stops me from fighting Egan's hair styling.

I scrunch my nose at Rosemary and open my mouth to talk to her, but she jumps up suddenly, pulling Aidan with her. "Let's dance, *Mo Chroí*. Join us when you're done, you two."

As they run off, I feel calloused fingertips skim the back of my neck as Egan gathers my hair. He bands it close to the base of my head, and my scalp gets a prickly feeling while he knots the ribbon.

Once he's done, he swings around me and steps down to the grass. He halts my hand when I reach back to feel the ponytail and instead wraps the second ribbon around my wrist, making an intricate knot of the ends.

"Are you ready to dance, Miss Sage? I want to enjoy as much time as possible with you tonight."

After I take his hand, we join in the revelry, dancing and laughing — and not once do I miss Ciaran.

Mam would probably say to be careful about appearances. But I don't believe I'm alone in thinking my relationship with Ciaran has run its course. I see no issues with making a new friend. I spend equal time dancing with other friends, like the son of my parents' neighbors, Murphy.

When the fire burns down to embers and the moon slides behind the horizon, Egan, Aidan, and Rosemary walk me through the Midding Gate. We are all tired as we walk the well-beaten path to my thatch-roofed bungalow, situated to the right of the incubation room.

I make a mental list of the things still left to do before the trip to Firehaven tomorrow. Most important is retrieving the eggs from the embers they lay in at night and transferring them into the special metal cages made for transport.

Rosemary hugs me at the door, and Aidan squeezes my hands before they bid me farewell, "*Slán go fóil*, Sage."

"*Dia duit*." I'm aware of Egan's large frame standing beside me as Rosemary and Aidan stroll arm in arm and linger at my front garden gate.

Slowly, Egan moves to stand in front of me. We've been talking and dancing all night, but now I feel awkward. I run my fingertips along the top of the knot at my wrist, avoiding Egan's eyes.

With one finger, he tips my chin up and bestows a sweet smile upon me.

"May I visit you in Firehaven? I wasn't kidding when I said I felt like you have me spellbound."

Bewildered, my gaze flits across his face before I look down and frown. No one has ever offered to visit me in Firehaven. Mam and Da won't brave the pass in winter, and Ciaran never even brought it up as an option.

Picking at the end of the ribbon at my wrist, I realize that my relationship with Ciaran is truly over. Whatever was there before, has withered and died from inattention. The fact that Egan is here with me at the end of the night and not Ciaran, speaks volumes.

The tips of Egan's black boots retreat from my vision, and I realize I've taken too long to answer.

I reach out and grab the sleeve of his leather cloak before he can back away. "I would love for you to come visit. No one has ever come to see me before. It could be an adventure."

A broad smile takes over Egan's face at my response. "I like adventures. Perhaps I can travel there to escort you back for the wedding?"

"Yes." I nod my head, "I would love for you to visit. And we could see where this," I wave my hand between us, "might go? We need to go slow, I just ended a relationship, and while I am drawn to you, I think it best we take our time."

Egan gently picks up my hands and kisses my knuckles. "Slow. We'll take it slow. I can do that. May I have the ribbon from your hair? A memento of our evening together?"

"Yes." I hastily pull the end of the ribbon and hold it by either end. But when Egan goes to take it, I pull it back. "Let me tie it on your wrist as you did mine."

"Miss Sage . . ." He seems reluctant, but I'm sure. This feels right.

My hands wrap the ribbon around his wrist two times before I start knotting it. I make it decorative, and he ends up with a knot that looks like a dragon wing.

Satisfied, I grin and ask, "Do you like it?"

"I do, Miss Sage, but—" I cut him off again. I can't seem to control my words.

"I wish mine would stay, but I know the first time I take a bath or get too close to a fire it will be lost." I sigh, already mourning the loss of my wrist decoration.

"If . . . if you're sure, Miss Sage, I can bespell them," Egan speaks slowly but firmly.

Looking into his blazing eyes, I see need and desire and happiness. I can feel it enveloping me, and the words slip out, "I'm sure. I'm sure I never want it to come unraveled."

Egan's gaze sweeps over my face before he looks down and takes my left forearm in the grasp of his left hand. Our ribbons are touching, and I grasp his forearm in turn. Placing his right hand over the ribbons, he gives me one last questioning look.

"I'm ready, Egan." And I am. Whatever this is, I want it.

"Put your hand atop mine, Sage. You'll know when to release it." As soon as my palm rests on Egan's hand, he speaks, "Bind and Stay, so mote it be."

Warmth encompasses my wrist and hand as words are pulled from my lips, "Stay and Bind, so mote it be." There's a sharp, searing pain at my wrist and then a cool wash of peace originates from that point and washes over my body.

I don't know how long we stand like that. I'm lost in Egan's gaze until a sharp gasp draws my attention.

Rosemary and Aidan have returned and stand to look down in awe at our arms.

Emblazoned along the top of my wrist is a red, orange, and yellow flame tattoo where the ribbon was. Along Egan's wrist is a red and black set of dragon wings.

"Oh, Sage." Rosemary tears up and looks at me. Whispering, she puts an arm around my waist. "Do you know what you've done?"

"I did what was right. I had to do it, Rosemary. I felt driven, compelled almost to say the words."

Shaking her head, she looks at where Aidan has pulled Egan off to the side. They are having a whispered argument. Aidan emphatically points at the tattoo and then at me.

"Aidan!" I stride over and stand between the two men. "I may not have magic, but I know when something is *right*. I live my life trusting my gut due to my lack of powers, and it has never led me wrong."

"But you're bound. You've bound yourself to a man you just met tonight!" While Aidan rants and paces, I step to Egan and hold his hand.

"Aidan! Stop!" Once I have his attention, I speak to my three companions. "Mam always told me the Goddess allows the magic to flow. And She doesn't make mistakes. Do you understand, Aidan? I don't know exactly what a bond is, but if the Goddess allowed this bond to be formed, then there is a reason. We'll deal with the fallout together."

I glance at Egan, and he gently enfolds me in his arms.

"Together," he repeats.

Oh, Goddess, what are you doing?

4

Morning came, as morning often does, way too early. The sunlight peeking through the mountain pass casts sparkles on the ice-coated grass. The day after Samhain always brings a light frost, and I enjoy the sound of the ice breaking underfoot as I make my way to the incubation room.

"Good morn, Master Riordan." I greet my boss as I switch out my leather cloak for a leather apron and long leather gloves.

Master Riordan has pulled our travel wagon into the middle aisle of the dragon stalls and hands me the base of a traveling cage. "Good morn, Miss Sage. I felt a wash of magic in the yard after the festival last night. Would you know anything about that?"

Halting at the half wall, I sheepishly peek over my shoulder, "I do. But I must speak to Mam and Da before I share it with you. They should be here soon, so you won't have to wait long for my news."

I continue on my path outside, opening the outer gate to the furnace.

The stomping of feet sounds behind us, and we both turn towards the Midding Gate. A young boy with tawny brown hair is being led forward by a much larger man. The boy is Renny, our new intern.

Holding the youngster by the collar of a sheepskin-lined cloak is my friend Murphy, Renny's older brother.

Murphy is a teacher and must have taken the day off to bring his brother for his first true day as an intern. I frown at the hold he has on Renny, though.

"Murphy, let the boy go." Turning to Renny, I smile encouragingly. "Good morn, Renny. I know this is the last thing you want to be doing. But chin up, you will be going on an adventure that your friends may never go on."

His blue eyes spark with interest, but he fights to keep a frown on his face. "Doubt it will be much of an adventure, tending a fire all day."

I gasp in mock horror. "Tend the fire? Do you think your job is to tend the fire? That's *my* job, thank you very much. No, you will have the privilege of handling the dragon eggs, in and out of lava pools. You will be luxuriating in the hot springs in the dead of winter, playing with dragons." I scoff. "Tending the fire, indeed."

Placing a hand on Renny's shoulder, I look between him and Murphy, "Unless, of course, your brother has promised you a different adventure? Maybe toting buckets of water in for his elemental class? Or perhaps, feeding the animals for the hexing professors?"

Patting his shoulder, I nod my head then turn back to the furnace. I place my first cage on the lip of the door, grab the metal scoop and fill the bottom of the cage with burning embers. The males stand behind me silently. Then I reach both hands in and pull out the first dragon egg. I angle it in plain view, so Renny can see the way the normally black eggs glow orange from the heat of the furnace. As I gently place it in its cage, I offhandedly address Murphy.

"Thanks for bringing Renny, but I think he'd rather stay with you than learn my boring job." I hand off the cage to Master Riordan to cap and wait for him to hand me the next one. Fully turning to Renny, I say, "Thanks for coming out, Renny. There are still two more eggs to prepare for transport, so . . ." I trail off as I observe Renny peeking into the furnace then glancing at his brother.

Taking a bold step forward, he states, "If you have gloves that will fit me, I would like to help you, Miss Sage."

Master Riordan chuckles, then leads the young boy away to get outfitted in protective gear for his first handling of a dragon egg.

Carefully closing the gate, I turn to wait for their return and realize that Murphy is inspecting me with amusement. Over his shoulder, I see my parents and Ciaran arriving. My parents look worried, and Ciaran is clenching his fists in anger.

Despite the inappropriateness of having a personal discussion in front of an audience, Ciaran bites out, "I have waited two years for you to hold up your portion of our relationship. But your refusal to network with me last night, and your continuing refusal to give me a dragon is beyond the pale. And then I find out about you and Egan. You don't even know him. Yet, last night. . . .

"Nevertheless, I need you in my life." Ciaran glances at my parents then does a double-take when he realizes his colleague Murphy has witnessed his ridiculousness.

"Walk me to the gate, Sage. You owe me that."

Pushing off, I walk ahead of him, eager for him to depart. Ciaran grabs my upper arm in a punishing grip and forces us to walk faster. For the first time, I notice how red his face is and the panting breaths he is taking, not from exertion but from anger.

Standing by the gate, I shiver as a bitter wind blows through and storm clouds start rolling in. Ciaran rips my glove off my right hand then forcibly holds my hand down on the Midding Gate. It's so sudden, I freeze.

"You *will* get me a dragon this year, Sage." As cold raindrops hit our hands, I flinch from the sting and the crazy, icy look I can see in Ciaran's eye. My heart races as it occurs to me that he is someone to be feared. I've forgotten that he is a powerful Warlock.

Thunder rolls in the distance as I tell him the only answer I have. "No. That has never been something I can control." I strive to keep my voice even, but I'm honestly terrified of my ex-boyfriend at this moment.

"So be it." Ciaran quickly binds my hand to the gate. "I heard you bonded with that man. If it's a bonding you want, it's a bonding you'll get. With me." Behind me, over the thunder, I can hear Murphy and my parents yelling.

Placing his hand over mine, Ciaran begins to chant. I tug futilely to disengage my hand, especially when his words penetrate the terror fogging my mind.

I want you to cower
You without power
My spell you will not sway

The Midding Gate
Becomes your fate
It shall bar your way

Until such time
A dragon is mine
Behind it, you will stay

A blinding flash of lightning and boom of thunder almost drown out his shout, but I hear it.

So mote it be!

The spell burns away the binding cloth, and as I fall back, the last thing I see is the ripple of power that flows from the Midding Gate and along the stone border wall.

5

"That was a blatant misuse of your powers, Ciaran!" Every other word out of Murphy's mouth is accented by a thud.

There's a slight ringing in my ears as consciousness returns. My mam's familiar scent of pumpkin and nutmeg fills the air around me as she gently strokes my bangs out of my face. She is weeping and soothing me, before gently helping me to sit up when she notices I'm awake.

The first sight that greets me is hard to swallow.

Murphy is sitting astride Ciaran, delivering punch after punch to the prostrate man. Ciaran has a bloody nose, a cut along his upper lip, and swelling under his left eye. The last punch knocks him unconscious. As I watch, Murphy pulls the leather band from his hair and muttering to himself begins binding my ex-boyfriend's wrists together.

"Dimwit. . . . Didn't even. . . . Poor choice . . ." The muttering continues with each loop of the leather and pull of a knot. With one last tug, Murphy addresses me, "How are ya', Love? That spell packed a wallop."

Pushing aside his dark-blond hair, I press a thankful hand to his cheek. "I'm well, my friend. Surprised . . . shocked . . ." tilting my head back, I let the rain soak me and with a small laugh, tease, "Wet."

"Aye. This storm is a surprise. Now, your da has left to get the council, but in the meantime . . ." Murphy places a hand in mine, the other on my upper arm and gently pulls me to my feet. "Let's get you somewhere dry while we wait. I'll come back for the dimwit."

I steady myself against Murphy, pausing briefly to pick up my leather glove which Ciaran tossed so carelessly to the side. It's slightly damp, but I tug it on. The biting rain gives me shivers as I'm wearing only a long-sleeved tunic and canvas trousers.

Mam nestles up to my left side and wraps the excess material of her cloak around my shoulders. Together, she and Murphy take me to my home, settling me in an armchair by my cold hearth.

"Go get Ciaran, Murphy. I'll start a fire directly and start some tea." Mam uses a quick flick of the wrist and a murmured spell to start a fire, while I hastily divest myself of the gloves and make sure that my sleeves are pulled down. I've not had time to speak to her and Da about my binding.

Murphy returns with Ciaran over a shoulder, and he wastes no time laying him on the floor at my feet. I raise an inquisitive brow, and Murphy replies to my unasked question.

"He doesn't need to be damaging your furniture, Love. He's drenched." He squats in front of me and starts untying my boots. "Let's get these wet things off of you."

His right hand is caught up in the laces of my left boot when Ciaran starts groaning. Reaching over to Ciaran's bindings, he chants. "Bind and stay, so mote it be." Ciaran's bonds take on a fused wet-leather look.

Impulsively, I lay my hand over Murphy's at my boot and complete the spell, "Stay and bind, so mote it be."

A flash of heat, and I'm caught in a familiar cool wave of peace as I stare into Murphy's blue-green eyes.

Goddess! I've done it again. What is wrong with me?

"Oh, dear. Oh, dear. Sage. Murphy." Mam's babble cuts through the fog of my mind. She's entered my sitting room with two mugs, steam spiraling lazily out of the tops.

I cut my eyes to her, witnessing a horrified expression on her face. "This should not be possible!!"

"The Goddess controls the spells, Mistress Ivy. I accept Her blessing." Murphy reassures my mam before pulling off my boot which is now missing its lacings. The top of his right hand is emblazoned with a set of blue and black dragon wings. Pulling off my boot, he eases the top of my purple fuzzy sock down to reveal a white, teal, and dark-blue wave tattoo along my left ankle.

"But a binding. I've not seen one since I was a child. No one is ever sure why the Goddess bestows that blessing — and to bestow it on my Sage? I've never heard of a Mundane being bound." Mam twists her hands together, worry evident in her posture and in the strain around her grey eyes.

Sheepishly, I look from Mam to Murphy, "Is now a good time to tell you that this is my *second* binding?"

"A second binding? Did my binding take at the Midding Gate, Sage?" Ciaran's voice is weak and slurred, but he's gaining strength and struggling to stand up.

"What? No!" I emphatically deny that I've made a binding with Ciaran. "Is that what the spell was about? You truly tried to bind me?" Aghast, I stare at Ciaran and wonder if I ever really knew him.

"Dearheart, if you've not been bound to Ciaran than who is the second binding with?" Mam hands me a mug of tea and perches on the edge of my side table. "Are you sure it was a binding?"

The mug of tea is not doing a great job of hiding my flushed face from my mam, and I take a small sip to buy some time. Lowering it, I cradle the mug in both my hands and in a soft voice admit, "Egan. The new blacksmith, his name is Egan, and we were bound after the bonfire last night."

A rap on the door stops further conversation. Murphy opens the door to reveal Da, Elder Thyme, and an agitated Egan on my small stoop.

Egan rushes to my side as soon as they cross the threshold. Clad in his work leathers over a tan sleeveless tunic and black canvas trousers, it is obvious he left straight from the smithy. Placing his left hand on my wrist, Egan takes a shuddering breath before kneeling on the floor by my chair.

"Miss Sage, I was so worried. I heard a tremendous 'boom,' and I could sense you were in distress." He tips his head to my shoulder, taking another deep breath and the anxiety I was feeling lowers a notch. "What happened?"

"I, too, am curious about that wash of magic." Elder Thyme glides in and takes a seat on my sofa, lowering her hood and giving a stern look Ciaran's way.

My ex-boyfriend glares around the room before mutinously staring at me, refusing to say a word.

"Twas an abuse of his magic, it was. And like the dimwit he is, he's bungled it." Murphy's strident voice fills my small sitting room. "He meant to keep Sage this side of the Midding Gate until he was given a dragon. But he has spelled the entire Midding fence."

Elder Thyme gives one slow blink and when her lashes rise, her focus has switched from Ciaran to Murphy. "Explain."

"He wrote his own spell, but in recitation, instead of saying 'you, without power' which would have focused the spell on Sage, he said 'you without power.' I fear, that all Mundane will be stuck this side of the Midding Gate." Murphy's jaw clenches in anger, "This includes my brother, Renny, and Master Riordan."

"I fear that it is more complicated than that." Several deep thuds sound from outside as Elder Thyme speaks. "The dragons are arriving. We were sent news they were on their way." Addressing Ciaran, her voice is stern and lecturing. "By stating particularly 'the Midding Gate' you, sir, have made that the only entry point to the dragon lands. There are five dragons living with fair champions. Five dragons that are now restricted from their villages. Because, in case you have forgotten, Professor Ciaran, dragons have no magic."

Even with Egan's and Murphy's calming presence, I become agitated. All I know about dragons flows through my mind. Utmost on my mind is that the creatures *need* their champions. A dragon and a champion have a symbiotic bond. The magic flows from the champion enabling the dragon to live further from their natural home of Firehaven. In turn, it loops back to the champion giving them a new magical ability.

If the dragons are restricted to this side of the Midding, their champions must live here, too. If not, the creatures are likely to return to Firehaven.

Pounding on the door stalls any reply I could think of. Once again, Murphy takes the initiative to open the door. Renny runs in, caught between excitement, anxiety, and fear.

"Miss Sage, the dragons! Master Riordan says you must come. The dragons and their champions are asking questions, and he needs your help." Wide, teal eyes target Murphy as he continues in a voice that cracks in his excitement. "Murph, you need to see them. Dragons, Murph, real live dragons. I've never seen them this close."

Handing my mug off to my mam, I stuff my feet back into my boots, frowning at the missing lace. Egan digs into the pocket of his apron producing a long strip of leather.

"You tie that one, and I'll work on this one." With a shy smile, he sets to work, giving me a hand up once we're done.

My worry about Ciaran's spell and my two bindings is overshadowed by the reality of two possibly angry dragons. "It's probably best if you keep a distance from the dragons for now, though if one of you could go see about having some sides of venison or beef brought over, that would be very helpful." Slapping my gloves back on, I gather Renny by the shoulders and steer him out the door. "Come, Renny. It seems adventure has come to us."

The ground trembles as two massive black creatures wander the grounds. Our coven stables the champions' dragons on the other side of the village. They help protect and guard our shoreline against predators. While they are of considerable size, they are small for dragons. I watch as they tentatively probe the fence line with a raised claw. It looks as though they are poking the air above the stone border, but the digits visibly fold back as they encounter the magical ward.

To my right, Master Riordan is talking with the two champions of my coven, pointing to the various homes on the property. As he points towards mine, he notices Renny and me and crooks a finger at us to go to him.

Keeping Renny within arm's reach, I pick my way across the yard. I want to make sure each dragon is aware of my positioning. Dragons are feral creatures. As such, I respect that any one of these creatures could take offense to either Renny or me and squash us like a bug.

Some ancient Witch formed an accord with the creatures. The dragons allow a binding and a cooperative relationship with their Witch or Warlock.

"Renny, the dragons will respect you if you show no fear. This means giving them space and making no sudden movements."

Ideally, I would have liked to ease the young intern into a meeting of the dragons. But we do not have that luxury, and the poor boy has been thrown into the deep end.

Approaching Master Riordan, I greet Laurel and Connell before introducing Renny.

"Miss Sage, thank the Goddess, do you know what is happening? We were feeding our girls when they raised their heads and started ambling this way." I love that Laurel calls the female dragons 'girls.' "They could not be deterred, and now it appears there is a ward on the border."

"There *is* a ward, courtesy of Ciaran." Facing the border, three more dragons come into view beyond the practice yard. "If you don't mind, let's wait until the others arrive, so I only have to share the news once. Elder Thyme is here, and I'm sure she will have more information as well."

I have just finished speaking when three dragons glide in. They are elegant and smooth, but despite that, there is a visible tremble of the ground and loud thuds as each lands close to the stable.

Steam rises from their flared nostrils as they stomp around, occasionally sniffing the ground then the air as if searching for something in particular. Only one dragon is relaxed. A massive dragon with silver tipping the edges of his wings, horns, and tail, lays curled beside the furnace. His hindquarters are curled to the side, his front legs crossed with his chin resting on top.

I take a moment to admire the glassy, obsidian-like scales on the majestic creatures in front of me. Three champions stride forward, all in various states of dress and all very angry. They are all familiar. Being champions, Master Riordan had me help deliver their dragons when they won their respective fairs.

They are all fairly large men, but the champion from Craobhan towers over the other two. It's almost impossible *not* to stare at the eye-catching Warlock. He has long, blond hair tied back with a leather band, green eyes, and his dragon must have tried to leave before he was dressed because he is clad in trousers and boots, but noticeably missing a shirt. He must have just had time to grab his cloak, for the blue wool of an Enforcer ripples behind him. I would think him handsome if not for the scowl and clenched jaw he's aiming our way.

"Good morning," Master Riordan greets the new arrivals then pointing our way continues, "Cathmor, Ronan, Dermot if you recall this is Miss Sage, and this is our newest intern, Renny."

Cathmor, the scowler, gives us a curt nod before demanding, "Why have our dragons been called? There was no missive, no forewarning that we needed to come to Lámhach. Is there trouble? An emergency?"

Settling against the half wall by the furnace, I lean back with my arms braced on the stones. "Are you familiar with Professor Ciaran?" Ronan and Dermot shake their heads 'no,' but Laurel, Connell, and Cathmor nod 'yes.' "Ciaran has been under the impression that I have the power to give the dragons to anyone I choose. Obviously, I cannot. In his anger, Ciaran has bespelled the Midding Gate and the entire wall. It was not well done, and instead of isolating *me* to this side of the border he has managed to exile all those without power. This includes your dragons."

The five champions cry out in anger, but Laurel's softer voice prevails. "What does that mean for us? Do we lose our dragons? Are we expected to live on this side with them?"

"I honestly don't know, Laurel. Elder Thyme is here, and I believe we are waiting for the rest of the council as well. I expect that shelters, if not homes, will need to be built soon. Master Riordan, Renny, and I are the only Mundanes in our coven. But I anticipate that Mundanes from Craobhan and Farrige will be arriving as soon as they can get transport. Are there many more Mundanes?"

Ronan — or is it Dermot?— responds, "We have two in Farrige. Though one was originally from Craobhan."

In a steely voice, Cathmor adds, "That is correct. There are no Mundane in our coven."

For some reason, that fact rubs me the wrong way. "There are no Mundane in your Coven *right now*? Or are you saying that Mundane are not allowed in your coven?"

Cathmor gives me a once over and evades a direct answer. "We have no jobs that a Mundane can do, unlike Farriage or here. The Mundanes travel to where the work is."

"I find it hard to believe—" I am cut off by Master Riordan.

"Sage, let's tend to the dragons. There is no use debating this when for the immediate future, all Mundanes will be living this side of the Midding Gate."

Bowing to his logic, I give Cathmor a scathing look then gather Renny to me.

"Let's see if we can put some fresh hay down in the stalls. My da is having meat delivered soon, and the dragons will want a dry spot tonight." Stopping before the first stall, I turn back to Master Riordan, "What will we do about our trip to Firehaven? The eggs will need to be placed in the lava pools soon."

"We'll make decisions after the council has deliberated and we know what the fallout is." Shaking his head, he looks out at the dragons wandering the land and the five champions who have seen Elder Thyme and are walking her way. "I'm glad that you and Ciaran are no longer together. There was always something about his eyes. He never quite met mine when we would talk, and I hated the way he patronized you for being a Mundane."

I let Master Riordan's words marinate in my mind as Renny and I throw hay in the stalls and add water to the long trough outside. Our work takes twice as long, as Renny gawks and stumbles, amazed by the beautiful creatures. And they are beautiful. It's amazing the various shades of black that are represented.

Throwing a glance towards my home, I see a crowd gathering at the door. As curious as I am about what discussion is occurring, I keep my focus on the dragons and their needs. It's my comfort zone, the edges of the action, relying on others more capable to deal with the bespelled border and Ciaran's abuse of power.

6

"Miss Sage!"

I jog towards the Midding Gate to meet Cian, the butcher, who is floating five sides of beef behind him. My intent is to open the gate and direct him towards a feeding area.

But I've forgotten the ward.

A foot away from the gate I run into an invisible mass, rebounding and landing flat on my back. My nose and cheek sting, my bottom feels bruised, and my pride takes a hit. Laughter rings across the yard, and I know . . . *I just know* . . . that the deep, booming laugh belongs to Cathmor.

Goddess. Why, Ciaran, why? Rubbing a hand at the pinch in my chest, I tightly close my eyes and allow myself a minute to grieve. Too many things are happening at once, but I won't cry. Taking two deep, deep breaths I will the tears away.

Focus on the dragons. There will be time to sort everything else out once the dragons are fed. Then I can focus on the ward and the bonding and that prejudiced . . . *Warlock*.

Once I have my emotions under control, I focus on the fence again through my peripheral vision. Cian does a flick of the first two fingers of his right hand, and the gate magically opens. Propping myself up on the palms of my hands, I greet him then wave to the right.

"If you could just drop them over by the last house, Cian, and maybe space them out? Perhaps every four feet or so? I'll get the dragons situated once you are finished."

Wiping my nose, I glance at the red that wets my knuckles, wiping it off on the side of my trousers. Blushing furiously, I wait for my face to cool down and hope the redness has disappeared when I turn back to the crowd outside my house.

Egan and Murphy are striding towards me, both with looks of concern. I wave them off, not wanting any more attention called to me.

"I'm fine. Let me get the dragons fed, and I'll join you. Renny!" I call the youngster to my side. Standing, I keep an eye on each dragon and while their nostrils flare at the smell of the meat, they remain by the stalls.

He takes a wide loop around the large creatures and keeping them in his sight, hastens to my side. "Yes, Miss Sage?"

"Here's your first lesson. The alpha dragon will be given the first choice at the beef, then the two females, then the two males. Which do you think is the Alpha?"

"The silvertip?" Renny points at the largest of the dragons.

"Yes, then the smallest are the females. Would you like to approach the silvertip with me?"

All covens are familiar with dragons. But very few are actually brave enough to interact with them. Renny will need to become accustomed to their presence, but five at once is understandably daunting. The most I've been around is three at a time, and while I'm confident, I don't want to push my young intern.

"Can I . . .? Is it alright if I stand with Master Riordan? I don't think I'm ready to be that close."

Clapping him on the shoulder, I give him a reassuring smile. "It's fine. I learned with only one here in the yard." I glance around, "Don't tell anyone, but I almost cried, I was that scared. You're doing great. Much braver than I with five dragons here."

Renny gives me a broad smile then backs up, "Thank you, Miss

Sage. I'll just be over there." He points towards my house before loping off.

Squaring my shoulders, I approach Cian, thanking him for the meat and then turn to the silvertip. With a confident stride, I make eye contact, keeping my breaths even and making no unnecessary movements. I've almost reached him when a bellow startles me.

"Stay away from my dragon, girl!"

Keeping eye contact with the silvertip, I slow my stride before doing a half turn in Cathmor's direction. At his shout, the silvertip has started to slowly rise, steam curling out of his nostrils, and his wings giving slight flutters as though he is ready to unfold them.

"I know what I'm doing, Cathmor. Your dragon needs to eat. Please let me do my job." My attempt to remain calm is belied by the strain in my voice.

"He's temperamental. You'll get hurt." Cathmor's voice is coming closer, but my full attention has been captured by the rumble emanating from the alpha dragon.

Standing stock-still, I warily watch the creature's advance.

"Miss Sage, slowly take a step towards me. He won't harm me, and I can protect you." Cathmor's voice is steel and ice. It slices through me and pricks my pride.

The snort I make is rude and unladylike. I know dragons. They are intimidating, but not once have I been scared of one. I have a healthy respect for the damage that one can do, but confident in my abilities, I meet the slitted, purple eye of the alpha.

The silvertip bares his teeth, and if I'm not mistaken, he is grinning.

"Miss Sage, now!" That bellow draws my gaze back to Cathmor. He's stopped several feet away, one hand clenched, the other outstretched, wiggling fingers at me to go to his side.

A moment of hesitation is all it takes. The alpha takes one more step forward, and I'm suddenly in the shade of the beast. Two large forelegs, taller than the top of my head are on either side of me. Cathmor's eyes widen as he raises both arms, waving them in a spell pattern. Whatever he's doing is not necessary.

"No, Cathmor, it's alright. He won't hurt me." To prove my point, I turn fully into the silvertip and lay both of my hands upon his scaled underbelly.

Slowly, gently, one clawed foot rises and tenderly wraps around my waist. The grip is strong but soft as I'm lifted high, higher, and then deposited on the shoulder of the beast.

My heart thunders in my chest. Never has a dragon lifted me. Never has one willingly borne the weight of anyone other than a champion. I'm equal parts thrilled and anxious at this turn of events. I feel a light tap of a claw on my thigh nudging me closer to the dragon's neck, and I grab hold of the smaller dinner plate-sized scales there.

Looking down from this considerable height, I see Egan and Murphy standing beside Cathmor. My two bondmates look on in awe, while Cathmor has fury written all over his face. Renny peeks out from behind his brother, eyes wide in excitement.

The silvertip turns ever so slowly and ambles over to the beef. Lowering his massive head, he sniffs at two before choosing a third. The ride for me is smooth, and though his scales are rough, they do no damage.

Like a big cat, he spins, then lowers his hindquarters to the ground. Stretching out his paws, he elongates his spine before curling in on himself. His spiked tail swishes once through the air before landing with a thud beside his feet. A deep growl emits from his maw, and the two females separate themselves and pad over for a meal. Once they've chosen their beef, the last two dragons stride over and take the last two carcasses.

Have you ever watched a dragon eat? I don't suggest it. There are bits of bone and meat flying and a lot of slobber. Hot saliva is dripping and steaming on the cold, winter ground.

Shifting, I look across the yard to see that most of the group now stands closer to the gate. Master Riordan and Renny are entering the stalls, I assume to tend to the eggs. But Ciaran is being led in my direction by Cathmor. My ex-boyfriend's wrists are still bound together, and I can hear his protestations carrying across the yard.

"I will abide by the council's decisions, but I don't know why I can't reside in Sage's cottage. She is mine, despite the bindings. *She is mine.*"

The derision in Cathmor's voice is unmistakable. "If you think the girl is going to want you in her home, or remain in a relationship with you, you are more misguided than I thought. You think you deserve a noble creature like a dragon? Neither Sage nor the dragons are possessions." Cathmor escorts Ciaran right to the silvertip. "Look my Onyx in the eye and prove your worth."

Ciaran strains against the hold Cathmor has on his arm, eyes wide with fear. His whole body trembles when the silvertip's tail rises and loops around his waist. The beast lifts Ciaran — exhibiting none of the gentleness he showed me — and stuffs Ciaran in the water trough.

And then I hear something I've never heard before. Dragons laughing. At least that's what I'm labeling it as. They are huffing quickly, the sides of their lips curled up with just a slight show of the razor-sharp teeth enclosed within.

7

I can't help the peals of laughter from slipping past my lips. Let's be honest, I don't try to hold them back. Ciaran deserves the humiliation. His botched spell has caused problems that I'm sure we are not even aware of yet, so I don't feel bad about finding humor in the situation. In fact, the look of fury on Ciaran's face only makes me laugh harder.

Unfortunately, I forgot my precarious position on the silvertip's shoulder and start sliding. I've only just started scrabbling for purchase when large hands grab me around the waist, and I find myself plastered against a naked chest before Cathmor unceremoniously lets go. Stumbling for a second, I grab at his arm to steady myself. Once I'm certain I have my footing, I pinch the large man just below the rib cage.

"You don't have to be so rough!"

"You touched my dragon! You call yourself a dragon tender and then you dare touch my Onyx without permission." Cathmor turns and towers over me, going for intimidation. But he's nothing compared to a dragon, and I poke the large man in the sternum.

"Is there a spell to correct your vision? The alpha picked me up. I did not climb onto his shoulder. Get your attitude under control." This man truly infuriates me. It's obvious he has no love for Mundanes, but he doesn't even respect my job as a dragon tender.

Shaking my head, I spin around and start walking towards the Midding Gate, determined to ignore Cathmor. Soon enough, we'll be off to Firehaven and will leave all this mess behind.

"Girl, I am not done talking with you." I can feel his presence behind me and walk a little faster, relieved to see Egan and Murphy heading in my direction.

"Miss Sage are you quite all right?" Egan grips my hand and pulls me into a hug.

"All right then, Love?" Murphy places a kiss on my temple but is giving a stern glare at the larger man coming up behind me. Ever since we were children, he has been protective of me, and the familiar touch is a comfort right now.

"Everything is well. Walk me to the gate? I heard Ciaran mention that the council made a decision. I'd like to hear more from Elder Thyme." Keeping my back to Cathmor, I straighten my spine, take the arms of each of my bondmates and continue on with the hope that I won't have to deal with either Cathmor or Ciaran much longer.

※

Elder Thyme steps forward and gently holds the tips of my fingers in her hands. "Sage, this is all grossly unfair to you and to the other Mundanes. We have tried to untangle the spell, but Ciaran is uncooperative, and I'm afraid we'll have to study and see if others might be able to reverse it. It is not all bad news." She gives me a strained smile. It's obvious that there isn't really anything good about this situation. "Though you, Master Riordan, and Renny may not pass through the Midding Gate, your friends and loved ones can. Rosemary's mother, Prim, has been using her crystal ball to keep in touch with the other covens. We have two more Mundane making their way here."

Releasing my hands, she turns to the others in our group, then sets her sights on Cathmor. "I understand this occurred earlier than planned, Cathmor, but you were moving here, anyway. We have sent a message to your father and explained the situation. Sage's parents have stated that you and Padraig can stay at their home until other accommodations become available. We welcome you and your father to our coven."

Cathmor's deep voice rings out from beside Murphy, "Father is almost ready for the move. I will travel back to help him bring our belongings here. He and I have experience building homes, I would like permission to build a small cottage on this side of the gate. I would prefer not to be separated from my dragon for any large amount of time."

Lowering my lashes, I peek at Cathmor with my peripheral vision. *This* is Padraig's son? *This obnoxious, frustrating man* is who my da was considering for me? It will break my da's heart when I tell him how unsuitable we are for each other.

Sighing, the questions I have been holding back tumble from my lips, "What are Ciaran's consequences? And what do my *bindings* mean? Will we be leaving for Firehaven tomorrow?"

Elder Thyme's focus on Ciaran causes all of us to look in his direction. He has climbed out of the water trough and is stomping towards the one lone empty house. Her voice is taut with frustration and censor. "He wants a dragon. He can earn one, and if the dragon accepts him, he can bond one. I'm sorry, Sage, but he will be required to go to Firehaven with you. He will be an intern and learn to do your job. His powers have been sealed until you return."

"Elder Thyme, I don't mean to question your judgement, but *this* is his consequence? It feels more like I am being disciplined for Ciaran's behavior." Huffing, I hold back the anger and keep my voice steady. "In five months, if he performs as an intern to Master Riordan, he gains a dragon? If he makes the journey to Firehaven and the hot springs with us, you believe he'll *deserve* one of these beautiful creatures? Without the trials?"

"Sage, dear. The important word in all of this is 'if.' Ciaran will be doing a Mundane's job without the use of his powers. You know him best. This will definitely be a trial for him. If at any point, he turns around or refuses to work, he will not have earned the right to a dragon."

She gives me a smirk, and I notice the twinkle in her eye. "I honestly don't think he'll succeed. But it will be a good lesson for him to realize he cannot just take or force things. He must work for them."

She doesn't think he'll be able to abide by his consequences. After seeing the fear he had of the alpha, Onyx, I agree.

Groaning, I pinch the bridge of my nose. Ciaran will make this whole process so much harder. "So, four of us will be leaving tomorrow?"

Laurel grabs my attention when she speaks, "We — Connell, Dermot, Ronan, and I — have agreed to teach Renny how to tend to our dragons. When you return, he will be proficient in dragon handling. We all felt that his and Murphy's parents might be relieved if he stayed behind since Murphy will be traveling with you."

"Wait. Murphy?" Confused I look at the man in question and see a huge smile spreading across his face.

"Your bondmates need to remain in your vicinity for the next three months, Sage. Similar to the champions and their dragons, to reap the full benefits of the bond, it must be strengthened with familiarity. We will not know what those benefits are until they present themselves." Elder Thyme regards all of us, concern written all over her face. "If they present at all. I'll need to do some research, but I don't believe there's ever been a Warlock-Mundane bond, much less a Mundane who has bonded with *two* Warlocks," Elder Thyme shares.

I send a shy smile to Egan, "This means you will be coming as well?"

"Yes, Miss Sage. I am eager to see your work with the dragons. I hope you don't mind." Egan pulls on my ponytail with a wink and a smile.

"Yes, yes. Can we disperse now? The Mundane has her orders and her magic protection detail . . . where will we be staying tonight? I for one, would prefer to stay close to Onyx and I'd like to at least find a shirt before making sure my dragon is tended to." Cathmor's impatience has him barging into the conversation.

The nerve of this man!

Master Riordan answers with a twinkle in his eye. "You and the other champions will be bedding down in the stalls until other accommodations are ready. I believe Sage's parents have extended an invitation to you." He quirks an eyebrow at Cathmor, "There is, of course, the option of staying with Ciaran, but I'm not sure how well-kept the cottage is. Your choice, Cathmor."

The group disbands quickly after that. The champions walk to the village for clothes and other necessities, Egan and Murphy to make arrangements with their respective jobs, leaving me with my parents.

"Sage, dear," Mam tucks her arm through mine and strolls with me and my da back towards my cottage. "You've had a . . . momentous . . . twelve hours. How are you doing?"

Considering I've tried not to think about any of the things that have happened, it's not surprising that I don't answer right away. It isn't until Da has ushered us into my home that I look into Mam's grey eyes, so similar to mine, and break. As soon as my parents witness the tears leaking down my cheeks, they hustle me to my couch and press me to sit.

Mam enfolds me in her arms and gives orders to Da. "Eoin, tea, please. Perhaps with a dram of whiskey."

8

I was four the first and last time my mam cried about my status as a Mundane.
Until today.

Today, as I sit in the protective circle of my mam's arms, she cries with me. For being a Mundane, for having a sorry excuse for an ex-boyfriend who has exiled me from my friends and family, and for being bound twice without comprehending what was happening.

Da sits on my coffee table and hands us each a mug of tea. Clasping his hands between his knees and leaning towards me, he says, "Sweetness, I'm too old to be throttling anyone. But have no doubt, if it were possible for me to take them on, I would be putting the hurt on both Ciaran and Cathmor. As it is, I *will* be having words with both boys. Especially Cathmor. Padraig and his mam did not raise that boy to be so disrespectful. The tone and words he used . . . no one speaks to my daughter that way."

The thought of Da taking on the 'boys' — as he calls them — warms my heart. In truth, those two were the least of my worries. Ciaran will be my burden to bear, and the ward is most disturbing, but that is completely out of my hands. Even if I had magic, it sounds like I wouldn't be able to reverse it.

"Thanks, Da. I'm not worried about Cathmor. That pile of dragon dung will be here while I'm at Firehaven. He's not worth the effort. Ciaran, though . . . traveling with him will be tiresome. I doubt he'll like the accommodations while we're gone. Sleeping in a tent on the way will be uncomfortable, and I guarantee he'll hate it." Using the hand not holding a mug, I brush my tears away. "I *am* worried about the bonding. What if being Mundane hurts Egan's and Murphy's powers? What does it mean to be bound? Are we tied to each other for life? I don't even know much about Egan. And Murphy . . ." I frown at Mam and Da. "I know that his own parents need his help at the mill, and he'll be traveling with me for at least three months. How is that fair?"

Mam brushes my bangs out of my eyes before placing a hand on my knee. "Tell me again how that happened. How did you even know how to work the spell? From what I understand, the bonding is a gift and *never* occurs the same way. *There is no spell to learn.* It just happens. The only thing we *are* certain of is that it requires a physical binding of some sort."

Handing my mug to Da, I pull up the sleeve of my tunic, revealing my flame tattoo. "Egan and I spent yesterday evening together at the Samhain festival. We performed the Spell of Light and Renewal together, then spent the rest of the evening talking, dancing, laughing. He, Rosemary, and Aidan walked me home. He'd taken a ribbon from my hair and made a cute bracelet of sorts with a decorative knot." Rubbing at the colorful flame, I continue. "It was such a lovely evening. I wanted to remember it and when Egan asked if I wanted him to reinforce the knot, I said yes. I didn't want to forget."

Slowly, I pull my sleeve down and take each of my parents by the hand. "I don't know what happened. It was the same with Murphy. The words were . . . they just fell from my lips. I couldn't stop them from coming out if I tried. It was like something took over my speech." Tears fell once again as I beseeched my parents to understand how I had no control over the bindings.

"I believe you, dear. The Goddess does as the Goddess will. It is not for us to question." Wiping the tears from her eyes, Mam straightens and states in a no-nonsense tone. "Well, you'll have to make the best of it. You are a talented dragon tender, Sage. Ciaran may be difficult, but I have faith you can teach him or at least aid him in hatching a dragonling. Don't forget your bondmates will be there to act as a buffer." She runs a hand down my ponytail then adds, "Egan seems like a sweet young man, and very handsome. And Murphy has always been a good friend to you, protecting you in his way. Neither will let anything happen."

Mulling this over, I have to agree. "I'm just . . . overwhelmed. I had a late-night, woke up early . . . the nonsense with Ciaran and the bindings and the ward and to top it off . . ." I remember Cathmor and hesitantly address my da. "I know you were eager for me to meet Padraig's son. . . . I think we can all agree it didn't go well."

"Aye, it did not go well. Not at all. I am severely disappointed in that young man." His lips pull down, and he rubs the back of his neck. "Padraig will need to be informed. This won't be the last time the two of you will be thrown together. Not with them moving to the village."

Da's next words get lost in the rapid bangs sounding from my front door.

Hastily wiping my face, I straighten my tunic, pull my ponytail tight, and answer the door. I block the entrance when I find Ciaran darkening my doorstep.

"Ciaran. What brings you here?" I bite the words out, steeling my spine.

Holding up his still bound wrists, he tries to push past me. "I'm looking for Murphy, your *bondmate*. He needs to release my restraints. I also need someone to get clothes and supplies for me. The ward won't let me through since Elder Thyme bound my powers."

My da places his hands on my shoulders and gently moves me away from the door, only to turn and confront my ex-boyfriend.

"Sage cannot help you with any of that, boy. You'd best wait for Murphy to return from town. As for your things, Ivy and I will swing by and grab them for you." Da takes a slow step over the threshold, silently forcing Ciaran away from the door. "It's more than you deserve. What were you thinking, placing that spell? You claim to care for Sage, but all I see from you is manipulation and entitlement."

"She had no right to deny me a dragon! She's a Mundane! Everyone knows that she is the one that has been judging the Fairs. It's common knowledge that who she roots for is who is awarded a dragon." Ciaran turns flinty eyes my way. "Everyone watches as she stands at the Midding Gate while the trials occur. She rooted for Laurel, Ronan, Dermot, and Connell. And each one won. That is not a coincidence."

Da stands stunned, but I storm out, demanding, "What do you mean 'it's common knowledge'?"

"Don't play dumb, Sage. Do you think everyone is so nice to you because they *like* you? You're powerless. The only thing you have going for you is your control of the dragons."

The gasp behind me matches my own. While I stand speechless, I grasp tightly to Da's arm. His whole body tenses up, and his face turns an alarming shade of red.

Mam marches to Ciaran, takes him by the ear, and wrestles him out my garden gate. Her voice carries in the cold air, "That will be enough of that garbage, you vile man. That is my daughter you are speaking about so callously. She has been nothing but kind and gracious to you, and this is how you feel? Eoin may be willing to help you get your items, but I assure you, I am not. I'll contact your uncle Lennon, and he can deal with this matter. You will not — do you hear me? — *will not* give Sage grief on this trip."

Mam shuts my gate and glares at Ciaran, who is flushed red from anger and embarrassment.

"That won't be necessary." Coming up the path is a slim man with features similar to Ciaran. "My nephew will be on his best behavior. Miss Sage, Ivy, Eoin, I apologize for the grievous actions Ciaran has chosen. Come, Ciaran, show me your new abode. I have brought supplies for you. Let's chat, shall we?"

Mam and Da stand beside me as a now pale-faced Ciaran follows his uncle like a child caught misbehaving on the playground. Shoulders curled in, stomping across the yard, Ciaran turns and gives one last glare over his shoulder at me.

"Watch your back, Sage. I'm glad you'll have Murphy with you. This will not be the last of your problems with Ciaran." Da's voice is worried as he gently turns me back to my cottage.

Ciaran's spiteful words have wormed their way into my mind, and my self-esteem has taken a hit. I was made fun of as a child for not having powers, but no one has truly said unkind things to me about being Mundane in ages. Is that because they think I have control over who gets a dragon? Surely not?

But then I think of Cathmor, and the disdain he has for Mundanes. He hasn't even called me by my name. Not that I can remember.

Fighting against the self doubt, I wander to my backyard and forage in my garden for salad ingredients. Armed with my bounty, I pull an apple from a tree at the back and wander back to my kitchen.

The sounds of the dragons and their champions are a murmur on the wind, reminding me of my place in this coven. I'm a dragon tender. My parents love me, I have friends, and I have the dragons. My job is difficult, but I excel at what I do.

As I sit at my kitchen table, I continue my pep talk. Who cares what Ciaran and Cathmor think? Even if more people don't *really* like me, I don't need everyone to like me. Yes, I wish more of the coven was honest, but that has no bearing on the good things I have in life.

I can only be me. I'll focus on the positive, do my job and continue on because even without powers, I am a worthy Witch.

Now I just need to believe it.

9

An hour later, I pull a sweater over my tunic and grab my gloves. Carrying with me a little bit of fear and a lot of fake courage, I head for the stables to speak to Master Riordan. Laurel has her dragon and Renny situated by the water trough, one hand on the young intern's shoulder, the other pointing out something on her black's tail.

This bolsters my confidence, seeing a champion, who should be angry that her dragon is stuck on this side of the Midding Gate, taking Renny under her wing to teach him. I hope that Cathmor's attitude doesn't undermine her efforts. I'll need to speak to him before leaving for Firehaven. I don't want him hindering Renny's education.

As I approach the half wall, I peek over at the eggs. Master Riordan must have moved the eggs to warm by the wall. Running my hand over the rough stones, I remind myself to stoke the fire soon. The aisle of the stables is brightly lit, Egan floating a glass globe with a flame captured in it by his side. Sometimes I'm in awe of the way magic is wielded to make such wonderful things. My boots scuff along the worn boards and almost go unheard by the three men loading the supply wagon.

Egan is tossing items up to Murphy who is organizing the supplies in the wood and metal wagon. Murphy is the first to spot me, and he jumps down to meet me.

"Hey, Love. We're just getting our things situated for the trip." My old friend smiles down at me, and it's contagious. I can't help but lift my lips and smile back.

"Murph, are you ever in a bad mood?" I tease the big man, tipping my head back to meet his eyes.

"Aye, you'll find that mornings and I are not friends." Rubbing his bruised knuckles, he admits, "And you know I have a temper when someone tries to hurt you. But for the most part, I'm fairly easy-going."

Master Riordan steps to my side, Egan following behind. "Sage, with these new developments, I've had to reassess our plan for this year."

My brows pull down as I turn my attention to my boss. "Reassess? What do you . . .?" No! *No, no, no, no, no!* "Please tell me you're not leaving me to train Ciaran alone. Master Riordan, you wouldn't do that to me, would you? Would you?"

When Egan places his hands on my shoulders, calm washes over me, and I become aware of the tight grip I have on the edges of Master Riordan's cloak. So tight, he's bending towards me because I have pulled him down to stare right in his brown eyes.

Taking a deep breath, I acknowledge to myself that I'm shouting — *at my boss!* — and might be slightly hysterical.

Leaning back into Egan, I slowly release my grip, one finger at a time, noting the way the material has creased from the manic hold I had on it. Gently, I pat his chest a couple of times, while I try my best to get ahold of my emotions. This has been the most stressful couple of days.

"Sage, you're ready. You know the way to Firehaven and the hot springs. You are strong and more than capable to deal with any danger, and you'll have two Warlocks with you." Master Riordan nods at the men behind me before saying, "Not just any Warlocks, either, your bondmates. They will back you up. There is also the fact that Renny needs me more than you do. For all intents and purposes, Sage, you are a Dragon Master in your own right."

My heart swells at the compliment. This is what I've been working towards for fifteen years. I'm aware of the responsibility thrust on me. I just need the confidence to do this.

※

The rest of the afternoon is spent speaking with the champions and teaching Renny basic duties of dragon tending. Thankfully, Cathmor has taken his leave to help his father with moving into Lámhach village. Ciaran and his Uncle Lennon stepped out of the last cottage to load up my ex-boyfriend's bags, but they avoided everyone.

Lennon's looks my way are unsettling. I'm not sure if he's angry on Ciaran's behalf or if he just doesn't like me. I've only met him a couple of times, and he was coolly polite every time.

Murphy's parents swing by with dinner for everyone as the sun starts setting. Egan and I eat together, leaning on the warming wall to fight off the growing chill of the winter evening. Looking out into the yard, we watch as Murphy and Renny talk with their parents.

"Murphy says you used to be neighbors?" Egan opens the wrap on the last parchment packet to reveal lemon tarts.

Snatching one of the fragile treats, I nod at Egan's question. "Yes, we went to school together until I was twelve and lived next door to each other until I moved here at eighteen. He and Rosemary are my best friends."

"I envy him. I would have liked to have known young Sage. Do you think we would have been best friends, too?"

"I don't know. I wasn't in the normal classes. Murphy and Rosemary became my friends due to living near each other. I had other friends, but we didn't really associate outside of school. And once I started my internship at twelve, we didn't have a lot in common." Shrugging away the past, I inquire, "Did you have any Mundane friends?"

"Not friends, family. My cousin is Mundane and is on the way here now. I think you'll get along well with Jasmine. She helps me assemble jewelry and mans my parents' store." Egan stands and pulls me up beside him.

"Do you think she'll be here before we leave?"

"Goddess willing, they'll be here soon. It's a four-day trip, though. The urgency with which the dragons flew in. . . . I suspect they'll be traveling non-stop." Egan threads my hand through his elbow and proceeds to head in the direction of my cottage. "Let's bid farewell to Murphy's family."

We say goodnight to the champions and Master Riordan, before collecting Murphy and his brother. Together, we enter my cottage. I've always thought it was roomy and spacious, but with two large men and one growing boy, my home feels considerably smaller.

I give a quick tour of the house, pointing out the bathroom and my two guest rooms. I also point out my outdoor shower off the side door to Renny. I explain how I use it before entering the house most days to keep the dirt and smells out of the house.

"Laurel and Connell will be staying here with you. Learn as much as you can. I was proud that you were learning about Raven. She's a beautiful dragon and takes well to Witches and Warlocks. Maybe when I return, you'll have something new to teach me."

Renny's teal eyes, so like Murphy's, light up in wonder. "Do you think I'll learn something you don't know?"

"I'm positive. I learn new things all the time, Renny. It's just one of the things I love about being a dragon tender." I walk towards the back and grab his sleeve to make him follow me to my garden. "Here's my garden. You are all welcome to its bounty. You'll see my mom come by every now and then to tend it while I'm gone. Rabbits get in sometimes, so be sure to be watchful and shoo them away."

Renny nods seriously as he looks around. "Can I ask you a question, Sage? Are you going to marry Murphy?"

"Oh!" Flustered, I stick my hands in my pockets and amble back towards the cottage. "Are you asking because he and I are now bound?"

"Well, yes . . . but also because he's been in love with you for years. You should hear how he talks about your hair, and your eyes, and your bum—"

"Renny!" My back stoop vibrates as Murphy's large form bounds out the door, down the steps, and into the yard. "Your loose lips are killing me. Where's the loyalty, Ren?"

Rolling my lips, I bite them to keep the grin from overtaking my face. Peeking through my lashes, I'm amused at the pink tinging Murphy's cheeks and the tips of his ears.

"So . . . you like my . . . *hair*, Murphy?" it doesn't seem possible, but the pink floods down his jaw and neck, as my friend gives me an embarrassed shrug.

"Aye, well . . .," coughing and looking away, he continues, "you know you're a bonny lass, Sage."

A warm glow fills my chest as I gaze at Murphy and really *see* him. He's grown from a tall, scrawny boy with too many cowlicks to count, into a large, muscled man with long, unruly curls held back with a leather strip. He was the boy who put frogs in my cups and spiders in my hair. But he was always my staunchest supporter and ally.

Murphy finally meets my gaze, and for a moment, time stands still, and that sense of peace that I felt at our bonding fills me once again. I'm lost in memories of him and me growing up, when Renny disturbs our tension-filled gaze.

"So, does this mean you're getting married?" The young boy's determination is impressive.

"Marriage has not been mentioned, Renny. We are still learning about the bond and what it means. Besides, I am also bonded to Egan. Am I supposed to marry them both? I think it has more to do with magical abilities than romantic relationships." With one last glance at Murphy, I steer my intern into the cottage. "We have an early morning. Let's all get some sleep."

10

Waking in the dim light of early morning, I snuggle deeper into my down comforter. The temperature definitely dropped last night. We need to get through the pass before any significant snowfall. The snow not only makes the pass treacherous, but the lower temperatures will freeze the Lake of Sorrows. It's generally a great spot to fish and supply us with food for the day.

Stretching out, I ease my way out of the bed then strip the linens. I'll collect the others' bedding as well, so that it's clean and fresh for the champions who will be residing here while we're gone. Plan in place, I pull on a grey tunic overlaid with a maroon sweater. Next a pair of leggings with canvas trousers over for warmth. Thick wool socks follow, and I lace up my calf-high boots over my trousers. I tuck my gloves into my pocket as I leave my room.

The house is silent as I tread across the hall and knock on the guest-room doors. "Rise and shine, sleepyheads."

Murmurs are heard from the door on the right, then louder voices as I distinctly hear Murphy, "Get up, Ren! No lazing about."

The door on the left pops open, and Egan exits with a leather bag over one shoulder and black boots in hand.

"Good morn, Miss Sage."

"Morning, Egan. Maybe you could drop the Miss? You make me feel like one of the elders." Gathering my hair to the side I start to braid it, only for Egan to put a restraining hand on mine.

"Just a ponytail, please. Especially if I am dropping the Miss, Sage." Dropping his items, Egan quickly gathers my hair into a ponytail, fishes a band from his pocket and ties it off.

"Do you always travel with leather bands in your pockets?"

"I do. Most are bits that I've cut from jewelry I'm making. I've found innumerable uses for them. Though, seeing my leathers in your hair has been the most enjoyable use so far."

After he gathers his items again, we exit the hall and wait in the living room for the brothers to join us.

Rapid footsteps echo through the house as Renny runs past with Murphy fast on his heels. "Morning, Sage. Morning, Egan. Bye!" Renny is out the door, hair uncombed and cloak flapping behind him as he escapes out of the house.

Murphy sinks into a chair, staring in consternation at the boots he's dropped to the floor. "The little pest tied my laces together." With a heavy sigh, he leans over and starts picking at the knots. He pauses briefly and flashes me a tilted grin, "Morning, Love."

"Morning, Murph. I'm just going to grab the linens and set them to soak. Laurel and Connell will need to hang them, but at least I'll have them clean for them."

"Sage." Egan rises from his chair and approaches me, "Murphy and I will clean them if you remake the beds."

"You don't have to do that. You're my guests," I protest.

Murphy pipes in, huffing as he works a particularly tough knot, "We're your bondmates, Love. *Warlock* bondmates. With my water aptitude and Egan's fire, we'll have them done quickly."

A familiar pang pinches my chest, but I cover my jealousy with a thankful smile. These men can do in minutes what it would take me a day to accomplish. I don't mind the work, I'm used to it. But just once, I would like just a small bit of magic to ease my way.

"Thank you. While you're doing that, I'll put some coffee on. I have some cranberry muffins from your mother, Murphy, and some eggs to scramble. We can break our fast as soon as they're ready."

The sky is full of pink-tinged clouds as the sun spreads its rays across the dragon lands. A light dusting of snow has fallen during the night, and we follow Renny's footprints to the dragon stables.

Renny is bouncing from foot to foot clad in a too-large leather apron and long, leather gloves. "Can we move the eggs now? Master Riordan says we're just waiting for you."

Nodding, I trade my cloak for my leather apron and pick my own set of long leather gloves. Turning to my bondmates, I ask, "Would you like to help?"

"Yes."

"Aye."

Reaching back, I produce two more sets of gloves. Renny is placing the three metal carriers on the half wall when we approach. I open one and tilt my head to the intern. "Do you remember what I did yesterday?"

"Yes. Scoop embers in the bottom then carefully place an egg in the carrier." He looks to me for approval, which I happily give.

"Exactly. Here, I'll hold the carrier for you."

Renny reaches in with the metal scoop and deposits the embers, then hangs the scoop on its hook. Tentatively, he reaches in and with a beaming smile, extracts an egg with two hands. Reverently, he places it atop the embers then fits the lid snugly to seal in the heat.

"Excellent!" I hand off the metal cylinder to Renny, "Take this to Master Riordan to put on the wagon. He'll show you how to secure them. That's an important step. We don't want the eggs jostled about as we make our journey."

I lean on the half wall and watch as Renny gingerly walks to the wagon that has now been pulled into the yard between the stable and the cottage Ciaran is staying in.

Speaking of my ex-boyfriend, the door to the cottage opens, and

Ciaran and Lennon step out. Lennon has a stern look on his face, and while I can't hear them, it's obvious that Ciaran is angry. His face is screwed up in a scowl as he leans in, arms crossed, while speaking to his uncle.

Other than teaching Ciaran the ways of a dragon tender, he's not my problem. I dismiss the dynamics between him and his uncle and eye my bondmates. "Who's next?"

Egan steps forward and opens the furnace. "So, I grab some embers then place the egg in the carrier?"

"That's right. The dragon eggs are pretty hardy but they are still eggs, so be gentle." I take the lid off the next cylinder and wait as Egan transfers some embers to the base.

He hangs the scoop, then gives me a raised eyebrow before reaching in for an egg. I watch as the excitement on his face drains away and confusion takes over. Looking at me over his shoulder he asks, "Are they supposed to be slippery? I can't quite get a grip."

"What? That's not right. They're rough and easy to grasp." I've never had an issue picking up the eggs. Renny *just* picked one up and transferred it with no issues.

Egan steps back, his hair damp with sweat from standing by the furnace for so long. "Murphy, you give it a try."

Murphy steps up, pulling his gloves up and spreading his fingers to make sure they are on correctly. He reaches in and after several seconds grunts, "I can't pick it up. Every time I think I have a firm hold, it slips right back out."

Handing the carrier to Egan, I step closer and peer over Murphy's shoulder. "Show me."

He stretches both hands out, cupping them around an egg, and it slithers away. Placing a hand on his shoulder, I lean closer, "Try again."

Murphy's body is tense and his tone frustrated, "Aye, Love."

Once again, he reaches forward; cupping his left hand, he nudges and rolls an egg close to the furnace door. "Here we go." He places both hands around the egg, hesitates, then frowning turns his head towards mine. "Love, take your hand off of me, please."

As soon as I step back, the egg shoots out between his fingers.

Stepping back, he closes the furnace door and brushes the sweat off his brow. Rubbing the fingers of his left hand along the palm of his right, a small puddle of water forms in the dip of his palm. He rubs his hands together then with his wet palms runs his hands through his sweaty hair.

"I think . . . and this is just a theory . . . I think only Mundanes can pick up the eggs. When you had your hand on my shoulder, I could tell there was a difference in the hold I had on the egg. As soon as you moved, it slipped away."

Like I told Renny, I learn new things about the dragons as I work with them. This new development is something that will need to be explored, and we can definitely put Murphy's theory to the test while we're on the road. But if this holds true, this means that Ciaran may not be able to help me with the hatching. It makes the process harder, but not impossible.

"Well, it's something to deal with later. If each of you can hold a carrier, I'll transfer the eggs. Once they're secured, we can head for the pass." Egan and Murphy each take a cylinder while I complete the transfer.

I let them tote the carriers to the wagon where they hand them over one at a time to Renny. "I'll be back, I'm just going to check on the dragons and tell them goodbye. Can one of you collect Ciaran and let him know we're heading out?"

Walking the length of the stable, I tread the soft grass of the back pasture. Laying at random spots are the dragons. If not for the deep black color and the steam emitting from their long snouts, I would think that Master Riordan had set up a garden of statues.

I pass each one, stroking a wing, a horn, a tail — whatever is within my reach. "Goodbye for now. I'm sorry your routines have been disrupted. I'll take good care of the eggs and hatchlings. I'll bring you new friends when I return."

11

The thing about mountains is . . . they're huge, colossal, and they look deceptively close. It takes the rest of the morning and into the afternoon before we pass through the foothills and enter the pass.

During that time, Ciaran complains. He complains about the weather. He complains about the slow speed we are traveling. He complains about . . . everything. The only relief I get is when we enter the pass. The path narrows, and Murphy takes the lead. I follow in the wagon, while Egan and Ciaran bring up the rear.

The wind is brutal, sleet is coming down and stinging any exposed skin, like tiny little needles. When Murphy slows, I keep my pace until he is riding just to the left of my seat.

"I don't think we should stop!" Murphy hollers to be heard above the driving wind. "Hand me some bread and jerky, and I'll take it to Egan and Ciaran. Stay the course."

I don't bother to pull my scarf down to respond. Transferring the reins into one hand I reach into the basket and hand him some packets of food. The men each have water jugs hanging off their saddles to wash down their lunch, so I flick the reins to pull ahead of the men.

With one hand on the reins, I eat my supper, waving briefly at Egan as he takes Murphy's place in the lead.

The side of the pass is steep, and we've been traveling in shadow. But as the shadows lengthen and deepen, I know the sun is starting its descent, and we've not yet reached the halfway point where we'll camp for the night. I urge the horses faster, knowing how frigid it can get on this road. The tightening in my chest releases as I see the bend before the pond.

On the left is an expanse of grass, a pond nestled against the curve of the pass created by a trickling waterfall. As I pull the wagon onto the grass I admire the small glimpses of green from the moss on the stones. Even more color is visible along the small outcroppings bordering the tiny fall in the form of ferns, mushrooms, and wildflowers. The aches in my back and thighs need to be stretched out, but the tension headache of the journey seems to melt away at the sight.

Jumping down, I take care of the horses first. Unhitching them from the wagon and walking them to the pond for water. Someone, years ago, placed posts at intervals along the shore, and I secure the reins to one. Heading back to the wagon, I see that the men have dismounted and are taking the saddles off of their mounts.

"I have oats for the horses in the back. Ciaran, come help me put some in the feeders after you secure your horse." I pull out the feed bags before climbing into the back and opening the burlap sack of feed.

Murphy yells out to Ciaran, "I'll take your horse to the pond, go help Sage. Remember what I told you. Mind your attitude!"

Ciaran stomps over and grabs the two feedbags I've filled. He's biting his bottom lip, and his brow is dipped down in an obvious attempt at holding his tongue. I would love to know what my overprotective friend said to Ciaran. But honestly, I'm happy if he's managed to curb my ex-boyfriend's antics.

Once the horses are fed, rubbed down, and secured for the night, we slide the poles and large canvas tent from the leather loops on the side of the wagon where they have been hanging. Ciaran grumbles when I hand him a mallet and the spikes which will provide the needed tension for the lines of our shelter. Egan and Murphy erect the fabric and pole structure with their combined magic, while I demonstrate for Ciaran how to place the stakes and tie down the tension ropes.

By the time we are done, Ciaran has a mashed thumb, and his hands have welts from pulling the lines tight. Grumbling, he stomps into the large tent, looking around at the large space. The space that is empty because I would not allow Egan or Murphy to bring anything in.

"Sage! Where will we sleep? How will we keep warm when it's so drafty in here?" Ciaran's demands grate my nerves.

I count down from ten to one, hands braced on the side of the wagon, and when I feel like I won't yell at the man, I reach under the seat and gather my sword and bow. Slipping my quiver over my shoulder, I calmly state, "Come get your bedroll, Ciaran. Then you and I will go gather firewood, we need to get a fire going for the eggs. Egan, Murphy, please gather your supplies as well."

Leaning my weapons against the outside of the tent, I take the time to set up my bedroll to the right of the entrance. I point out where we'll build a fire tonight, right under the vent hole in the middle of the tent.

Ciaran continues to grumble as we gather firewood and as he struggles to light the fire with my flint and chert. We only get a reprieve when he finally settles on his bedroll against the back of the tent and falls asleep in exhaustion.

❧

It snowed during the night, and the guttering fire hisses as melting snow drips into the flames. There's always a muffled silence here in the glen after snowfall, partially due to the creatures being careful of icy conditions and partially due to the falls freezing.

The large thump and crunch outside the entrance flap has me scrambling for my sword. Ciaran remains rolled in his blankets. My bondmates, clad only in trousers and socks, are crouched on the other side of the fire beside their bedrolls.

A bright-orange flame is floating over Egan's left hand, his right swirling and gathering sparks from our campfire. Murphy is in a similar position but trickles of water are flowing up from the ground and a spiral of water levitates over his left hand.

There are many wild animals out here, bears, wolves, griffins . . . trolls. *Oh, Goddess, please don't let it be a troll.*

Stealthily, Egan motions me forward and mouths, "Untie the flaps." He positions himself in front of the entrance as I reach for the leather strips and pull . . . one, two, three, four. Bending, I take a firm hold of the flap, sword at the ready, and nod to my bondmates.

Throwing the canvas back, we are met with a swishing, scaled tail. A familiar tail, tipped with silver spikes. Onyx is sitting outside our tent.

Lowering my sword, I shove my feet in my boots and swirl my cloak over my shoulders. When I step out, my bondmates are beside me, hands still glowing with power, but their offensive spells have disappeared.

Groaning, I search for Cathmor, unsure why the champion and his dragon would have followed us into the pass.

"Egan, do you see Cathmor?" I keep my voice pitched low, not wanting to surprise Onyx as we slowly work our way around the massive creature.

Onyx is staring north down the pass, snout tipped up and sniffing the air. It reminds me of how the two females were sniffing the ward at the Midding Gate. Whatever he smells is not visible, and I have no true way of communicating with the dragon.

Once he's reassured that there's no immediate danger, Murphy retreats back into the tent. Egan sidles up beside me and gazes up at Onyx.

"Cathmor is not here. What is the dragon doing? Why is he here?" Egan tilts his head towards me and his breath tingles across my ear as he quizzes me.

Placing a hand on the warm scales of Onyx's leg, I turn a puzzled look at Egan. "I'm as confused as you are. It doesn't bode well that he's here without his champion. He might fly back to the stables when we continue on, let's break our fast and pack up. We have to get the eggs to Firehaven. Onyx will do what he will."

12

What Onyx does is continue on our journey with us. Sometimes flying ahead, sometimes hopping from ledge to ledge as we traverse, like a playful, oversized bird.

The snow has slowed our journey, the wheels of the wagon needing to constantly be cleared of ice build-up. Egan easily takes on this chore, his hands glowing with an orange light as he periodically runs them over the wheels to melt the ice with his fire magic.

We awkwardly eat lunch on the road, not daring to pull off our gloves or expose our faces for too long to the elements. I don't want to delay our journey. Once out of the pass, the snow will peter off the closer we get to Firehaven and the volcano that feeds the lava pools.

Ciaran has taken the lead, bundled head to knee in furs. I envy him. It is so cold, my fingers are stiff in my kid gloves, and my cheeks feel raw from the constant blowing of the cold wind. Only a few more miles to the lake, and then we can shelter in warmth.

When the Lake of Sorrows finally comes into view, the mid-afternoon sun reflecting off the minute ripples of the surface blinds me. We've come through the pass unscathed, and I take in the frost-covered grass, the long, low wooden hut where we will rest tonight and the stone-rimmed fire pit where we shelter the eggs.

I slide more than climb off of the high seat of the wagon, leaning heavily against the side as I stretch out my legs and bend back to loosen my spine. In my peripheral vision, I see the men dismounting with a little more pep.

Onyx circles overhead before landing on a boulder beside the lake. As I go about caring for the horses, I glance over every now and then. The dragon has his head tilted down and is inspecting the water. Curious. I've secured the horses into the open-air stalls to the left of our shelter when I hear a splash and a plop.

"He's fishing." Murphy sidles up beside me and tilts his head to Onyx.

"He is swift. Dips his claws in and pulls out a fish." Egan has a grin on his face as he passes us with his mount. "I thought we'd be freezing by the shore fishing later."

"We still might. A dragon eats a lot, Egan. We'll see if he'll share." I return to the wagon to find Ciaran weaving his hands for a spell, then giving a huff when he remembers his magic is bound, before reaching for the feed bags. I startle my ex-boyfriend when I speak up behind him. "How are you doing, Ciaran?"

"Things are so much easier to do with magic." He huffs. "I understand why you were always so tired." He gives me a forced smile.

Helping him fill the bags, I pause and ask, "Ciaran, seriously, why are you set on getting a dragon? You've disrupted a lot of lives. Is this worth it?"

"You wouldn't understand, Sage." Gathering the loops in hand, he starts to step back, but I grab his arm.

"Ciaran, you've always put me off when I asked in the past. What are you hiding?"

That was the wrong thing to say. Ciaran rips his arm from my grasp and strides angrily away.

Brow furrowed in confusion, I determine to get an answer from him soon. But first, I need to do my job. Twisting, I release the latches on the first carrier to carry it to the fire pit.

Egan has started a fire, and I gently place the metal cylinder on a stone of the fire ring. Pulling my long gloves from the inner pocket of my cloak, I prepare to remove the egg.

"Ciaran! Grab your gloves and a carrier. We need to transfer the eggs!"

But, as has happened all too frequently, nothing goes to plan. Even with his magic bound, Ciaran can't touch the eggs. Unlike Egan and Murphy who got a grasp on them, the eggs seem to create a barrier six inches from the surface.

"Why can't I hold them? I thought for sure with my powers bound I'd be able to grasp one. Nothing is going as planned. If I can't hold these, how will I ever hold . . .?" Ciaran slams his mouth shut and looks wildly at each of us.

Murphy growls in the back of his throat and steps to Ciaran's side. Egan's eyes are slitted, and his head is tilted as he inspects the other man, as if he could read my ex-boyfriend's thoughts if he glares hard enough. I'm just confused.

"How will you ever hold *what*, Ciaran?" My demand is met with silence, and Ciaran attempts to walk away.

"No." Murphy places a heavy hand on Ciaran's shoulder. "She asked you a question."

"I'm here to learn and earn a dragon. I have no obligation to answer her questions. She is difficult and never appreciated that I was with her, a *Mundane*. I owe her nothing." Shrugging Murphy's hand off, he heads back to the wagon.

"He's up to something." Egan spells the fire higher before continuing, "Are there only these eggs? Or could he get some when we're in Firehaven on his own?"

Ciaran doesn't spare us a glance as he passes on the way to the shelter with his bedroll.

"He *could* find an egg in the wild. But I wouldn't want to take an egg from a dragon. The accord we have with the dragons is long-standing. Even once they hatch and are presented to the champion, they don't *have* to bond," I say, as I try to explain the ins and outs of the dragon bond. "The dragon has to agree. Sometimes, they don't deem the champion worthy and return to the dragon lands. They *allow* us to care for and hatch the eggs. It would be very dangerous to attempt to steal an egg in the wild."

The men nod quietly, musing over my words and what Ciaran could be possibly wanting.

"If you two have things handled out here, I'm going to get the rest of our bedrolls for tonight and some food." Murphy looks over my shoulder, "I think Onyx will be sharing some of his catch with us."

Egan and I turn in the direction of the lake to find Onyx gathering two large trout in one claw before he ambles in our direction. The rainbow trout lands with a plop in front of Egan before the big, black dragon does his catlike stretches and curls beside the fire.

Murphy drops off a food basket before continuing on to the low shelter. Pulling out serrated knives, Egan and I each set to cleaning and filleting our dinner.

Pointing his knife at Onyx, Egan asks, "What do you think is going on there? You know Cathmor can't be far behind."

Groaning, I wipe my bangs from my forehead with the back of my wrist. "I know. I am *not* looking forward to that confrontation. I wish I could talk to him."

"Cathmor?"

I tilt my head towards the dragon. "Onyx. I don't know how long he and Cathmor can be separated. And I hope. . . . I hope Onyx isn't trying to return to the wild."

Placing some butter in a pan, I let it melt while combining herbs and spices to add to our dinner. Egan tosses the fish heads to Onyx then starts chopping up some vegetables.

Hesitantly, I share my worries, "I'm out of my depth here. I'm so, so . . .furious . . . with Ciaran. I'm afraid my cheek is going to be a bloody mess by the end of his training. He'll do what I ask, but he's making no effort to learn or even help without prompting." Poking the fish with a cooking fork, I avoid eye contact with Egan, "I'm worried about our bonding. What if I hinder your magic in some way? I'm sorry. Goddess, I'm so sorry I did this to you, Egan. You're stuck with *me*. A Mundane. What happens when you want to marry? What if the border spell is never reversed? Are you stuck with me, this side of the Midding Gate? I just. . . . I'm-I'm so-sorry."

Calloused hands frame my face, and I lift a tear-blurred gaze to the raven-haired man before me. Gently, he wipes my tears with his thumbs, then places a kiss on my forehead.

"Shh, shh . . . everything will be fine. The Goddess knows what she's doing. We'll figure out what Ciaran has planned, deal with Cathmor if and when he shows up, and the bonds. . . . Sage, you have to know, the bond would not have taken if both of us didn't want it." Twirling a strand of my hair around his finger, Egan gives a guilty smile. "I may have just met you a couple of days ago, but Aidan and Rosemary have been sharing stories about you for weeks. I took full advantage of the festivities on Samhain that allowed me your company. We may not know what the bonds will do for us yet, but if the only thing that occurs is that I am bound to *you*, Sage, for life. . . . It is well worth it. *You* are well worth it."

13

"**G**irl! Where are you and where in the heavens is my dragon?" The bellowing voice wakes me from a wonderful dream of tiny dragonlings fluttering at my fingertips.

Sitting up drowsily, I grab a tunic and layer it over my sheer undershirt. As I pull my hair out from under the tunic, I tilt my head toward the closed door of my room.

"Girl! Where is Onyx?" Heavy footsteps resound from the main room, but also from the rooms on either side of mine — Egan and Murphy are up.

"Cathmor, it's the middle of the night. . . . No. Put the plants back outside." Murphy's voice is raspy as he reasons with Cathmor. I'm not sure what plants have to do with anything, but scuffling noises are now coming through the door.

Oh, for Goddess's sake!

Flinging my door open, I step into. . . . What have I stepped into? Egan and Murphy stand closest to me, hands outstretched, glowing balls of magic poised over their palms. Cathmor is several steps in from the open entrance door, vines creeping along the ground around him and winding up his arms. Oh, *plants,* Cathmor's magic must deal with plants.

Pushing past my bondmates, I head for Cathmor, only to trip over a vine and land on my hands and knees in front of the man.

"Pull them back, you pile of dragon dung," I hiss at Cathmor, as I sit back and inspect my foot. His damn vine had thorns and there are drops of blood on the tip of my toe and a long scratch along the top of my right foot.

The vines retreat as Egan rushes to my side. Murphy trots back to his room, gathering a bandage and a jar of salve before returning to my side. Cathmor continues to stand imposingly over us all.

"I want my dragon, girl," Cathmor growls out.

"Then go get him." I wave him off and point to the door. "He's obviously not here unless you think I've managed to hide him under my bed. There was no reason to come storming in here waking us all up at Goddess knows what time of night." I let Egan and Murphy help me off the floor before addressing the stubborn Warlock again. "He's fairly large, Cathmor. Last I saw of him, he was curled around the fire. You can't miss him."

This Warlock. I don't have time to deal with him. If he can take Onyx and *leave*, my life will have one less problem in it. But the way he's glaring at me — I don't think that's going to happen.

Wearily, Cathmor falls into a chair across from me. "He's not out there, and your fire is out."

The fire is out?

The eggs!

Running out the door, I cross the yard to the empty and cold fire ring.

The eggs and their carriers are gone.

No! Heart pounding, I gingerly hop-walk across the frozen ground, looking for any sign of the eggs.

"Come inside, Love. Get dressed, and we'll work out what's happened." Murphy lifts me up into his arms, getting my bare feet off the frosty ground and walking back to the shelter.

As we cross the threshold, Egan comes out of the fourth room. "Ciaran is gone. I'm sure if we inspect the wagon, we'll find things missing from there as well."

I only have one job. Take the eggs to Firehaven, help them hatch and grow. But I've failed. Like I always do. A Witch with no magic. A dragon tender with no dragon or eggs. Numb, I wait for Murphy to set me down before stumbling back to my room.

I'm so heartbroken.

"Sage!"

"Love!"

"Girl!"

Ignoring their calls, I drop to the bed, pull the covers over my head, and close my eyes. I just need a moment. Just one to wallow, before I carry on. Morning is soon enough to go after Ciaran and the eggs. I cover my sobs in my pillow, hoping the men can't hear me. I just need a moment.

※

Thump, thump, thump

"Sun's rising, girl! Get up!" Cathmor bangs on my door again. *Thump*

"Sage! The name's Sage, Warlock!" Sitting up makes my head hurt, and my eyes are puffy and sore from crying myself to sleep.

"I don't care! Get out here." There's scuffling from the main room and murmurs then Cathmor's loud, "No!"

Dressing quickly, I toss my bag over my shoulder and roll up my bedding. When I exit into the main room, Egan has Cathmor in a headlock and bent at the waist. Murphy is crouched in front of him, whispering harshly.

When my boots ring on the stone floor, the men spring apart. It would be funny if we weren't dealing with a missing Warlock, missing eggs, and a missing dragon.

"Morning, Love," Murphy whispers in my ear as he takes my bag and bedroll.

"Morning, Sage." Egan runs his fingers through my hair and deftly gathers it into a ponytail.

Cathmor growls at me, but reaches and takes my cloak off the hook by the door. Swinging it over my shoulders, he takes the time to secure it. This close, I can see the bruising under his eyes and the paleness of his complexion. He's feeling the effects of being apart from his dragon.

Hesitantly, I raise a hand to his face, "Cathmor, can you feel Onyx? At all? We'll get you two together soon."

Flinching away, he strides out the door. "Let's go, gi . . . Sage. Let's see what clues we can find now that the sun is rising."

Snow covers the ground, and without the heat of the day, stepping out into the cold is a shock to my system. Fisting the edges of my cloak from the inside, I tuck my chin in, attempting to keep warm.

Egan is poking at the ashes of the fire, while Murphy inventories the wagon. Cathmor takes a right out of the shelter towards the horses. As I approach, Egan sets a log into the fire ring, and with a flick of his wrist restarts the fire.

"Working on the assumption that Ciaran has stolen the eggs . . . I don't understand how he could have gathered them. I think we've effectively proven that only I can pick them up." I hold my hands over the flames, rubbing them together periodically, mulling over the mystery.

Handing me a mug of tea, Murphy wraps his arms around me, "Could he have nudged them in? Remember I was able to roll the egg even though I couldn't pick it up?"

Both hands cradling the mug, I let the steam warm my face and hide the blush that creeps into my cheeks at Murphy's closeness. "Maybe? Should we continue on to Firehaven? If he wants to hatch them, he'll have to head for the lava pools."

A sharp whistle pierces the air, then the sound of muffled hoof beats rumble across the ground. The sound has us looking in Cathmor's direction. Three horses come into view and slow before him, reins trailing through the snow.

"We have a decision to make. Ciaran released the horses, these are the only ones who have come back." Cathmor walks towards us leading the horses. "We can hitch the wagon and one of us rides. Or we take essentials and make better time on horseback."

I've been staring into the fire as he is speaking, and when I lift my head, I find all three men's eyes on me. *Oh!* They're letting me make the decision.

"Firehaven. We go to Firehaven on the horses, we need to catch up to Ciaran."

Before the men can move, there's a great flapping of wings, a burst of wind, and Onyx lands beside the lake. It's a clumsy landing, and he stumbles forward several steps before stopping much closer to where we stand by the fire. The reason for his awkwardness is immediately clear.

Safe within his claws are the dragon eggs.

14

I found something positive about having a bondmate. Egan is a blacksmith. This is fortuitous, since we need new carriers for the eggs. Ciaran may not have been able to take the eggs, but he took the metal cylinders that we used to transport them.

Murphy and I sort through the items on the wagon, while Egan works on new carriers. We make piles of what we need (food, my leathers for hatching the dragons), what we find useful (tools, tent), and things we can leave behind (duplicates, the wagon). Then we start making up three bags, one to be carried by each horse.

"Why are you separating the items?" Cathmor's sudden appearance surprises a shriek out of me.

"Three horses, three riders — we can each take a bag." I buckle my saddle bag and carry it to the horse I've chosen for my mount.

Cathmor's response is disbelieving. "Three? There are four of us. Onyx and I can carry quite a lot."

Resting my head on my saddle, I shake my head. "I assumed you and Onyx would return to Lámhach." Silence greets me.

Straightening, I look fully at Cathmor. He's standing with his hands on his hips, head turned toward the lake, brows pulled down.

When he speaks I can barely hear him, it's almost as though he's speaking to himself. "You don't know." His sudden turn and intense stare make me stumble back until the saddle bag digs into my spine.

This time his voice is louder and demanding. "You don't know, do you? You're not. . . . You haven't . . ." Pinching the bridge of his nose, he continues, "I owe you an apology, Daisy."

"Sage. The name's Sage." Seriously, I think I have a pretty easy name to remember.

"Do you not remember me? You were probably three when your da left you to stay with my folks. Your mam was sick, and they worried about you. Do you not remember?"

"No. But if I was three, I know the time you are talking about. My mam wasn't just sick, my baby brother, Keefe, was stillborn, and Mam hemorrhaged. I think I was too young to remember details clearly. I only know what I've been told." I try to remember that time of my life, but I only recall the oppressive grief that reigned in our house that summer. But *daisies* — I remember daisies.

Peering up at the large man in front of me I squint my eyes, trying to remember *him*. "I remember that was the summer I learned to make daisy chains."

"Aye." Cathmor's eyes travel from my face to the top of my head. "I was six, and I would make you crowns. I tried everything to keep you from crying. You were miserable being away from your family."

"If you knew . . . know who I am, why have you been so rude and dismissive towards me?" I can't make sense of his behavior.

Cathmor sighs, and his breath ruffles my bangs before he searches my eyes. For what, I don't know.

"Our folks have always wanted us to marry. It's one of the reasons my da wanted us to move to Lámhach. Have your parents not ever mentioned it?"

"Oh, my da might have mentioned you a time or two. But he just wanted us to meet. He never mentioned marriage," I reply.

Cathmor admits, "I thought this was all an elaborate ruse to force us together. But it's not, is it?"

"No. No, just a misguided boyfriend, who is doing something dangerous to get a dragon." Carefully easing around him, I remark,

"Besides, no Warlock will marry a Mundane. What could I possibly contribute to a marriage?"

"Daisy, you don't believe that do you?"

Giving a little fake laugh, I speed up, "Of course, I believe it. It's the truth. Don't act like you don't believe it, too. I've been on the receiving end of your derision for all things Mundane."

"Daisy, I . . . feck! Just because *I* don't want to marry doesn't mean there's not a man out there for you. For Goddess's sake, two men agreed to bind with you."

"A binding is not romance, it's not marriage. That's the truth of the matter." Goddess, I really don't want to talk about this.

"What's the truth?" Murphy is walking from his horse to the fire and giving Cathmor and me a curious glance.

"Daisy, sorry *Sage*, doesn't think anyone would want to marry her." Cathmor is hard on my heels as he answers Murphy.

"What? Fecking hell, Love, what put that notion into your head?" Now Murphy's striding closer, gaze fixed on my face.

"I *know*. Cathmor was saying that our *parents* want us to marry, and I was pointing out the obvious — how ridiculous that is. I mean I'm a Witch without powers. Who wants that? Who wants *me*? Ciaran proves that guys only hang out with me because of the dragons. It's all just . . ." I wave my arms around and stop mid-sentence.

Eager to end this discussion, I hurry to the fire to check on the eggs. Talk of marriage makes me uncomfortable. The familiar ache of rejection pinches my chest. I've always known that I would live my life to work and care for the dragons. I thought I'd resigned myself to it, but having bondmates gives birth to new heartaches. We're bound for *life*. I'll have to watch Egan and Murphy fall in love, marry, and have children — perhaps I'll be the eccentric aunt, teaching the children about dragons, making them daisy chains when they visit.

This is all so overwhelming. There's a reason I prefer to be on the fringes. I dislike confrontation and I get — itchy — when people get too close. I don't know how to deal with attention.

Scurrying past the fire where Egan's working, I bury my face in Onyx's expansive chest. The dragon settles lower to the ground and crosses his forelegs together, making a haven for me to shelter in. The sunlight is blocked out as with a dry rustle, he unfurls his wings and closes me in.

"What did you . . .?"

"You. . . . Insulting her. . . . Two days . . ."

". . . misunderstanding. . . . Apologized. . . ."

"Not good enough. . . ."

Only snippets of their argument float into my haven. Cocooned within Onyx's wings, I take several breaths. I can do this. Get the eggs to Firehaven. Find Ciaran and discover why he wants wild dragon eggs. It might be uncomfortable traveling with Egan, and Murphy, but if I set my mind to it, I can do it.

"Daisy, come out. Onyx, open up." Cathmor's deep voice is just the other side of the dragon's wings.

Taking several deep breaths, I stand and tap Onyx's breast. "You can let me out now. I'm okay. Thank you for letting me hide for just a minute."

With a whoosh, Onyx spreads his wings then with a flutter sets them flat against his back. Cathmor stands before me, one hand covering his mouth, one on his hip regarding me.

"Daisy."

"My. Name. Is. Sage." Pushing past him, I take several steps before I realize Egan and Murphy are warily watching me approach.

I can feel my cheeks heating, so I lift my hood to hide my blush. Pulling on my gloves, I address Egan, "Are the carriers ready?"

Egan tilts his head to the side, inspecting what little of my face he can see, "Yes, it's ready for you." He speaks slowly and softly. Rising, he rounds the fire ring and stands just in front of me.

Cradled in his hands is a large carrier, and it shows me just how talented he is. He only had to make three metal cylinders. Instead, he shows me one carrier with three separate slots. Along the sides and the handle are metal leaves; sage leaves, decoratively placed in an attractive pattern. Each closure is essentially a hasp, but he has molded them to resemble a bundle of sage.

Pushing my hood back, Egan looks into my eyes. "We would very much like . . ." He clears his throat and glances at Murphy, who steps up beside him. "It would please *us* if you would accept this gift and grant us permission to court you. If you are concerned, we gained permission from your da before we left."

Speechless, I stare at him then down to the carrier. Hesitantly, I take the gift from Egan then search his eyes. He's serious. Slightly turning my head to the left, I peek at Murphy. He's smiling and nodding at me.

"Is this? Is this a joke? Or . . . do you feel obligated because of the binding?" Frowning at the men, my heart skips a beat, thinking they are making fun of me.

Murphy brushes by Egan and takes the carrier from me, handing it back to my other bondmate. Gathering my hands in his, he gives me an earnest look. "Sage, Love. I asked your da months ago at Midsummer. I was waiting . . . hoping . . . that things would not work out with Ciaran." Brushing a gloved hand over my cheek, he takes a step closer. "Renny did not lie. I've loved you for a long time, Sage. Magic or no, I think you are a powerful woman. Everything you do, you accomplish without magic. That makes you *more* accomplished in my eyes. It always has."

Egan takes my free hand and just as earnestly states, "I've seen how hard life is for my cousin Jasmine as a Mundane. She's a wonderful woman, but she's bitter and angry all the time. You're not like that. You embrace who you are, and I will admit the bonding is part of why I want to court you." He tightens his grip when I go to pull away. "Not because I feel obligated, but because when I tied that ribbon on your wrist, it felt right. And when you asked me to spell it, all I could think was that I wanted to keep you. I'll forever be thankful the Goddess granted my wish."

Nodding, I grip their hands, "I-I believe you. Both of you. But . . . I need time to . . . adjust. So much has happened in the last couple of days. Life-changing things. But we can talk more as we travel?"

Broad smiles cover my bondmates' faces as they nod their agreement.

A loud clap sounds behind me. Cathmor. I'd forgotten about Cathmor.

"Well, now that Daisy is reassured that she is, indeed, wanted, let's pack up and get on the road." Cathmor strides past, grabs the carrier, then waits by the fire ring, pointing at the eggs. "Do you want to do the honors or have Onyx lift them?"

"You're coming with us?" Confused, I stalk over to the fire and pull my gloves on.

"It's what I do, Daisy."

"Sage." Why won't he call me by my name?

"Your job is to tend the dragons and the eggs. I'm an Enforcer for the covens. Mine is to carry out justice. And I believe, *Daisy,* that your ex-boyfriend definitely has some things to answer for."

15

Once the decision to move is made, you would think it would be a quick departure. But we did not count on an ornery dragon.

The dragon allows us to load him down with supplies, but when Cathmor tries to climb up, Onyx side steps. He, in fact, steps in such a fashion that I can't approach my horse.

"Onyx! We need to be on the road. You must allow me to climb on." Cathmor's frustration is echoed in his bellow as he makes demands of his dragon.

"Perhaps he would rather Sage rides him? He did follow her here, after all." Egan offers this suggestion, watching in bemusement as Cathmor and I dance around the dragon and are getting nowhere.

At his words, Onyx lays beside me, one purple eye staring at me with determination. With unsure steps, I look up the vast side of the dragon. "Is that what you want, Onyx?"

Cathmor grunts as the dragon's tail prevents him from getting close. "I'm just going to lift her up, you stubborn creature."

Relenting, Onyx lets Cathmor by. With steady hands, Cathmor lifts me by the waist and directs, "Sit between his spine ridges. One more back, so you're not accidentally hit by his wing."

After I'm situated, with a bit of fear about the height — and we're still on the ground — Cathmor heads towards my mount. His stride is heavier than usual and he's flexing his hands. He can't get close to my horse, though. Onyx deters him.

"What now?" Cathmor faces down his dragon, spine straight, hands on his hips and a scowl on his face. It's evident he's not happy that Onyx wants me to be his rider.

Onyx's tail whips out, grabs Cathmor and drops him behind me.

Twisting around, I watch as Cathmor stands on the dragon's back and situates himself behind me. I'm acutely aware of his thighs lined up behind mine and his chest nestled up against my back.

Taking a deep breath to steady my nerves, I smell . . . earth? Dirt? "Cathmor, why do you smell like my garden?"

"Do you know nothing of plant magic? I have live vines in my pocket. I need a base for my magic." We jostle against each other as Onyx rises to his full height.

"Alright then, Love?" Murphy yells up at me as he gathers the reins of my mount and ties them to his saddle.

"I'll have to be won't I? Unless you'd like to argue with a dragon?" I give him a wave and try to find a comfortable position. "Head east around the lake. The path to Firehaven will be marked. Hopefully, Onyx will keep us in eyesight as we travel."

That's all the conversation the dragon allows as he jumps and with a huge sweep of his wings launches us into the sky. The motion pushes me back into Cathmor, who in turn wraps an arm around my waist and grips the dragon's spinal ridge in front of me.

"Feck! Hold on, Daisy. Onyx's movements are large, and he can easily throw us off if you're not holding on."

Is he kidding? I don't want to fall off! With a gulp, I look down and see the lake growing smaller underneath us as Onyx loops around and around gaining altitude. Egan and Murphy are riding at a fast clip to the east, occasionally hazarding worried glances at us.

Soon, we're gliding in a zig-zag pattern, the dragon doing his best not to outpace the riders. And it's the best feeling in the world. My stomach has a tingly feeling that is not unpleasant. My cheeks are starting to hurt because I can't stop the smile that is affixed to my face, as well as from the biting wind chafing my skin.

We're making good time when I see an unfamiliar glimmer ahead, at the juncture of the lake and the start of the road to Firehaven. Squinting, I fight the glare that is now shining off the . . . wall. An ice wall!!!

"Cathmor!!! Get Onyx to turn, or stop, or something!" Screaming, I watch in horror as the wall of ice looms larger and larger in front of us. The form stretches out in either direction as far as I can see.

"I don't see anything." Cathmor is leaning over me and pounding with a fist on Onyx's shoulder blade.

With horror, I scramble for a handhold as Onyx halts mid-flight, perpendicular to the ground forcing Cathmor and me to lean forward. There's a terrible drumming sound as the dragon's extended wings catch air to halt our forward progression, and then a massive gust of wind crosses over his back as Onyx levels out and turns abruptly to the left. My body tumbles to the right and out of Cathmor's grasp.

And then, I'm weightless. My shriek is lost in the awful screech as Onyx's claw on his right wing scrapes against the wall. I fall back against Onyx's side before his hind leg clips me and sends me into the barrier. My cheek burns against the frozen ice before I bounce off and I am free falling. Closing my eyes against the wind, I'm only aware of my pulse pounding a rapid beat in my ears. My mouth dries out as I continue to yell.

Suddenly, I'm jerked, and I feel a tightness around my arms and torso. I finally dare to open my eyes. Two thick vines hang before me, and I track their length to Cathmor. He's straddling Onyx's tail both hands out, directing the vines to me and yelling.

"Bind and Stay! So mote it be!"

As I feel the vines tighten, I feel the words building in my throat. They want to come out. "Mmmph." Biting my lips, I deny the words that I feel compelled to say. Blood fills my mouth and tears burn my eyes as I fight the binding spell. I can't be bound to Cathmor. I won't. He would hate me.

Slowly, agonizingly slowly, Cathmor reels me in as Onyx drifts lower and lower to the ground. Cathmor has just grasped me in his arms when Onyx lands, and we roll off his tail onto the hard rocks of the road.

Gasping for breath, I lay on top of Cathmor. The retreat of the vines hisses across my body until it's just Cathmor's arms around me. He has one arm around my back, a hand on the back of my head, pressing it to his chest. His heart is pounding just as quick as mine, and he's trembling.

"I thought I lost you, Daisy. I almost didn't get the vines out in time. It was so close. Too close." His grip tightens, and he sits up keeping me in his hold, so I'm straddling his lap.

With far gentler hands than I attributed to the big man, Cathmor holds my head in both hands. Sorrow fills his green eyes as he scans my face. "You're bleeding. We need . . ." There's a hitch in his speech before he clears his throat and continues. "Can you stand? We need to get you cleaned up and bandage your cheek."

Except he doesn't let me up. He just continues to stare at me, and once again, I find myself engulfed in his arms. His words whisper across my hair, "I don't . . . I can't lose you."

16

Lunch is held on the side of the road around a small fire Egan magicked up. Each of us is staring in the direction of the wall, though only I can see it. Even several yards away, the ice wall shimmers and glints in the sun.

"There's a gash visible way up there where Onyx skimmed it, and I think that's your blood a little lower down." Cathmor points up and to the left with his piece of jerky, where a splash of blood is hanging, seemingly in mid-air. "You're lucky you only got a couple of scrapes the way you slid off it."

The others may be looking where I *luckily* just scraped the ice, but I'm studying the ground. There is no demarcation visible where the ice meets the road. "How could anyone even spell something that large?" I ask hoarsely, still strained from my screaming.

"Runes. Or a spelled object to anchor it. How far up could you see, Sage? Do you think we can fly over it?" Egan tosses his apple core to his horse and advances on the wall, one gloved hand held out.

"I only got the barest glimpse of what was above before I panicked, but I don't think we can fly over." Standing, I wince at the ache in my ribs and left leg. Between bouncing off of Onyx and the vines jerking on me, I am covered in abrasions and red spots that will surely be bruises in the morning.

Striding past Egan, I stop at the wall and run my hand across it. "It's smooth and cold. Can you feel it?"

The men gather and place their hands on the wall. Or at least that's what they attempt, because their hands go straight through. Egan actually stumbles forward and turning quickly stares at me from the other side.

Murphy and Cathmor each start to step through, but I put my arms out, holding them back. "Egan, can you come back across?"

Anticipating a barrier, Egan puts his hand through first before striding back to this side. "There's definitely a ward up. I felt the cold as I walked through."

With both hands, I bang on the barrier. No! "It's Ciaran's spell or something like it. You can go through, but I can't." I drop to my knees and think every bad word I've ever learned. "Feck! I can't even send you across with the eggs. The pools hold some kind of magic. The eggs have to be walked in because the carrier will melt."

"Do we have time to send for a council member? If Onyx and I fly back to Lámhach and bring back an Elder, perhaps they can bring this down if we can't?" I watch as Cathmor paces, hands behind his head, problem-solving.

"I don't know." Sitting back on my bottom, I curl my knees up to my chest and watch as Murphy walks through the barrier and back. "The hatching's already been delayed, and they've been in and out of fire more than I've tried doing before. I don't even know if they're viable anymore."

When Egan sees the tears coursing down my cheeks, he settles behind me and wraps me in his arms. Closing my eyes, I wipe my tears and straighten my legs. They're sore from my near-death experience, and I attempt to find a comfortable position.

"Daisy!"

"Sage!"

"Love! Look at your foot! Is it past the barrier?" Murphy squats by my foot, which is becoming increasingly numb and waves his hand over the space. "It's actually in the ward, isn't it? I can feel where the temperature changes just above your foot."

Egan jumps up to inspect, and immediately, my foot feels constricted and pain radiates up my leg. Hissing through the pain, I try to retract my foot. "It's stuck! I'm stuck in the ward."

Cathmor grabs my shoulder, "Try now."

Pulling at my leg with both hands I clench my teeth and grit out, "It's still stuck."

"The bond! Move, Cathmor. It takes our bond." Murphy lowers his hand to my foot and immediately the pressure eases. "I think Egan or I can pull her through the barrier with the power of our bond. Cathmor, see if Onyx can come through with yours."

Shaking his head, Cathmor disputes this reasoning. "He would have gone through earlier if that was the case."

"Not necessarily. He was carrying Sage who isn't bonded to either of you. If you had fallen instead of Sage, you most likely would have flown through the ward on your own." Egan eyes the dragon and the horses, both still by our fire. "We can only try Cathmor. We all need to get through."

We return to the fire, where Egan extinguishes it, and we load up our supplies. Approaching the ice wall, Egan and Murphy attempt to go through with the horses. The blacksmith and his horse travel through, but Murphy gets stuck when the eggs are stuck on this side.

Untying the carrier from Murphy's saddle, he continues on, and I watch as they secure their horses. When they return we all stare at the metal housing in my hands.

"Now what?" I ask.

"Hand me the eggs, Daisy." Cathmor reaches for the carrier then places a kiss on my temple. "Walk through with your bondmates. I think Onyx can carry the eggs through. The eggs should have some sort of bond with the dragon, aye?"

Hope bubbles in my chest that we might all make it through the ward. Together, we walk to the wall. Cathmor keeps one hand on his dragon, and they easily pass to the other side, eggs included.

Murphy and Egan each grab one of my hands, placing arms around me, and we slowly move forward. Shivers attack me as we enter the ward, and I strain against the thick, syrupy feeling of the ward. I'm completely within it when I realize I'm stuck. I can't take another step forward.

My bondmates tug, but it's no use. I can't cross over. The ward is too thick for me to walk through and too strong for Egan and Murphy to pull me out. My chest heaves as the ward fights me, and spots appear before my eyes the more I strain.

Helplessly, I stare at Cathmor on the other side and time seems to slow. Each breath is harder to take than the one before. Egan and Murphy stand at my sides, legs spread wide. Each has a hand behind my back pushing and another hand on my biceps pulling.

Cathmor stretches his hands out and vines crawl up out of his pockets, around his arms, and then they are slithering around my body. Leaning back, his muscles bulge against the strain.

Bind and Stay. So mote it Be!

The magic he instills into the vines crashes like a wave over me and again the urge to complete the binding washes over me. Biting hard against my already ragged lips, I hold the words in.

"What are you doing, Daisy? What's she doing?" Even as Cathmor yells, I can feel myself slogging forward.

"She's fighting the binding! This is exactly how she and I became bound, her reversing and stating the spell!" Murphy hollers back before telling me. "Let it out Love. Don't deny the Goddess."

Shaking my head, I bite harder and scream behind my lips. Slowly, the men get me through the border, and I collapse on the ground, panting heavily, blood trickling out of my mouth.

Cathmor jerks me off of the ground, roughly wiping the blood from my lips. "Stupid girl! Why were you fighting it?!"

Egan and Murphy jump forward to separate us, but Cathmor spins us out of their reach and shakes me. "Why, Daisy? Why?!"

Weakly, I push fruitlessly against Cathmor. "Because you don't want me! You don't like Mundanes! You would hate me if we were bound." Hiccuping through my tears, I wail, "I don't want to be bound to a man who would hate me for the rest of my life!"

Cathmor shudders, gripping my arms tighter before gathering me gently into his arms. "Oh, Daisy. I don't hate you." Rubbing small circles across my back, Cathmor tilts his head down and whispers in my ear, "I don't hate you. I don't dislike Mundanes. I was pushing you away. You deserve more than a man who is away more often than he is home as a mate."

What?

With one hand, Cathmor tilts my chin up and gives me a sad smile. "I've been in love with you since I was six years old. Once I became an Enforcer and I had business in Lámhach, I would see you. Always watching from the Midding Gate. I saw the way the kids loved you and the villagers would wave and smile when they passed you. I saw you, Daisy. *My Daisy.*" Cradling my cheek, he leans closer until all I see are his green eyes staring deeply into mine. "I don't want to hurt your poor lips, but I'm going to kiss you now."

Confused, I nod my head 'okay' and with my pulse-pounding and butterflies fighting in my stomach, I allow the big, arrogant jerk to kiss me.

His lips brush first one corner of my lips, then the other, before placing a firm but brief kiss upon my mouth. Pulling back, he scans my face looking for my reaction, but I think I'm in shock, and I can only stare back.

"I haven't talked with your da, but I think he'd approve. Will you allow me to court you as well?"

17

"I think you broke her," Murphy lobs that accusation to Cathmor.

"I didn't break her. Did I, Daisy?" Cathmor gives my waist a little squeeze from where he's seated behind me on my horse. I say behind me, but I'm really positioned over his thighs, we wouldn't have both fit on the horse otherwise.

Onyx decided no one would ride him. He is flying in spurts above us, landing every now and then to inspect a pond for fish or to chase butterflies in a field. Yes, the big dragon was trying to sneak up on butterflies.

"She's not usually very chatty, but she's never silent like this." Egan pulls alongside us and peers down at me. "You broke her."

"Feck off." Cathmor's hand disappears from my waist, and in my peripheral vision, I see him give Egan a shove. "I didn't break her."

Tuning in to the conversation, I say what I've been puzzling over since we crossed the ward.

"How did Ciaran get through? He's not bonded, and his magic is bound. So, he couldn't have walked through nor could he have set the ward."

The silence from the men is instant. The ring of hooves on stone and the jangle of the harnesses is all that can be heard as they digest the conundrum.

"Feck! He has help. Whatever he's up to, he has a Warlock or Witch helping him." Cathmor reins our mount to a stop and jumps off, which makes me land hard in the saddle.

"Ow. Bruised woman here. Aren't you supposed to be wooing me or something?" Grumpily, I rub my sore bottom.

Cathmor rolls his eyes and starts pacing.

"Think, Sage. What could he want? He wants a dragon but not one of the three eggs we have. Are there other dragons near Firehaven?" Egan has dismounted and taken hold of my reins. Standing beside me, he lays a hand on my thigh.

Furrowing my brow, I look down at him, then eye the other two. "Of course, there are other dragons. Larger, and more dangerous dragons. The great reds are fire breathers. They live at the top of the volcano. But trying to get one of their eggs is almost impossible."

"Impossible or improbable?" Egan gains my attention with his question.

"Very, very improbable." With Egan's help, I clamber down, feeling every bruise and scrape my body has incurred today. "The closer you get to the volcano, the more hostile the air. Sulfur is emitted and can kill you. I'm not sure you could reach their aerie even with magic. If the sulfur doesn't kill you, the heat will."

"There's something else. There has to be." Murphy motions everyone off of the road and into an adjoining field. "We bundled his things together. I didn't see anything interesting when I was packing it, but let's go through it all."

Egan and Cathmor are rummaging through the scant belongings Ciaran left behind. Murphy and I have decided to go hunting for dinner. We're in a valley between the mountains, hunting small game.

"There." Whispering, I stop Murphy and aim for the twitching ears rising above the grass. There's a soft twang as I let my arrow fly, swiftly followed by another as Murphy spots a second set of ears, just to the left.

Wild hare is not my favorite meat. But we need the fresh game; jerky and unleavened bread make for a poor diet. Advancing on the bodies, I slide my knife from my boot and start skinning the coarse-haired animal. Murphy and I have hunted together since we were in our teens and have a routine. Side by side, we gut the hares, leaving the innards and heads for other animals, we take the hearts for Onyx.

Bundling the meaty hares, Murphy sets them to the side then starts twirling a finger over my palms. Water gathers, and I'm able to wash off my hands. After doing the same for himself, Murphy picks up our dinner, then clasps my hand in his and leads us back to the side of the road.

"How are you really, Love?" he asks.

"Confused. I thought I knew what my life was — is — but the past three days have. . . . I'm having a hard time believing . . ." Flustered I wave my hand around, "I keep thinking I'm going to wake up. That this is all just a wild dream." Raising my hand to the bandage on my cheek, I confess, "If not for the aches and pains, I could imagine that I'm still sleeping in my bed. Safe and sure of life in Lámhach."

Murphy pulls me closer and still holding my hand guides them behind my back. "Is it a bad dream?" Concern shines from his teal eyes as he scans my face.

Lifting my free hand to his collar, I finger the frayed edges. "No. There are some bad portions, but you and Egan and even Cathmor make it good. Great, even. Unbelievable, but great." I try a smile, and because it's Murphy, I rise onto my toes and place a kiss on his lips.

It was meant to be a swift, friendly kiss, but Murphy hauls me higher and presses a warm, firm mouth against mine, sucking my lower lip in between his. The hares land with a thump on the ground as he releases them to free his hand.

Tingles run through my body as he cups my cheek in his hand and licks the seam of my lips. When I gasp, he takes advantage of the moment and deepens the kiss.

I run my hands into the back of his hair, pulling, arching into him, wanting to sink into him. With a groan, Murphy grips my thighs and secures me around his hips. His trousers do nothing to hide his arousal, and for a moment, I forget everything. Ciaran, the eggs, my bruised body — it all fades away as I'm focused solely on my bondmate and the heat rising in my body.

Dimly, I hear a cough and a chuckle. Panting, Murphy slows the kiss and rests his forehead on mine. When I open my eyes, I take a deep breath to steady my heart, and I realize Egan is standing beside us. With a smile, he tugs on my ponytail and whispers, "I'm sorry to disturb you. We need to eat and get on the road."

Lowering me to the ground, Murphy growls at Egan, "You're not sorry. Jealous perhaps, but not sorry." Giving me a gentle smile, he sets me away from him and starts adjusting our clothes. Somehow, he'd managed to untuck my undershirt and release the laces at my neck. Murphy is likewise disheveled, and I blush when I notice at some point, I'd completely unbuttoned his shirt, and his muscled chest is on full display.

Egan smirks and gathers me to his side. "Not jealous. *Mo Chroí* appears very . . . happy. I don't have a problem sharing her with you." Speaking low in my ear, he states, just for me, "Don't be embarrassed, we're already sharing a bond. If you want Murphy, or me or Cathmor . . . or all of us . . . I'm willing to do what it takes to keep you happy."

On that note, we return to Cathmor. Murphy with a very proud grin on his face, Egan and I walking hand in hand. Cathmor studies my flushed face and swollen lips, then glances between Egan and Murphy. "Doing well then, Daisy?"

Lifting my eyes to meet his, I make a show of fixing my hair and doing up the laces of my shirt. "Very well. Thank you for asking, Cathmor."

Ciaran's items are tossed haphazardly on the ground, but from here I can see a bit of paper in Cathmor's hand. He offers it to me with a carefully blank expression, "Does this make sense to you?"

The scrap of paper is ragged on the edge, like it was torn from a book. It contains a short list.

Bond with Sage
Travel to Firehaven

Gather elementals
Spell - bond
Council

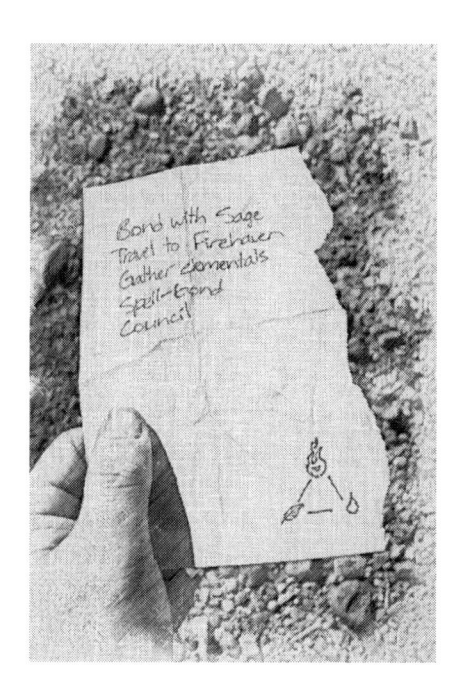

Tracing the familiar writing, I read the list three times. "Elementals? Does he need the three elements for a spell? Is it a special bonding spell?" Tapping the last item I slant the scrap, so Cathmor can see it, "And this? Council? Does this mean the council knows what he's doing?"

"I know what he's doing." Murphy's sure voice is brimming with anger, "There's a legend — a folktale, really, about three powerful elemental dragons. It has many versions, but because he mentioned the bonding. . . . There is only one that has a bonding requirement.

"A Warlock and his bondmate must travel together through fire to acquire the mythical dragon eggs. A sacrifice must be made before the eggs can be touched. Presumably, great power is transferred to the holder of the eggs." Shaking his head Murphy laughs, "I'm not sure if I even remember the details correctly. Ciaran's a fool, chasing a child's tale."

Rereading the list, fear grips my heart. "He wants the dragons for power. The only reason he would include the council . . . he wouldn't try to overthrow the council would he?"

"I think that's exactly what he wants. If he truly believes the tale . . .," Cathmor stops and stares into the fire, "He has just become a very dangerous individual."

18

Our conversation goes round and round as we prepare and eat dinner. The truth of the matter is that we won't know for sure what's going through Ciaran's mind until we catch up with him.

We eat quickly, packing up to make the most of the daylight. Sunset is still hours away, but on a normal trip, we would have already been in Firehaven. Cathmor takes the lead, two swords crossed behind his back and knives tucked in various holsters on his thighs and wrists. Now he looks like the Enforcer that I would see at a distance occasionally in Lámhach.

I'm doubled up with Murphy, enjoying the way his biceps rub against mine as he confidently holds the reins in one hand. His other hand rests carelessly across my thigh. His thighs bunch occasionally beneath mine, as he uses his knees to control the animal below us. It's intimate and comforting within his hold, and I continue to remind myself to be vigilant of danger.

Egan rides up beside us, cloak discarded as the weather warms the closer we travel to Firehaven. "Have you seen Onyx? I've noticed Cathmor searching the skies, but the beast has not been in view since dinner."

"I wouldn't worry too much. He's probably off hunting down his own dinner." I'm confident that is where he is, but I, too, tip my head back. The sky is streaked with pinks and oranges as sunset approaches, with only a puffy cloud dotted here and there against the blue expanse.

"Whoa!" Murphy pulls back on the reins, and my eyes are drawn to the trail ahead of us.

Cathmor dismounts, knife in his right hand and his left outreached to something hidden by trees. Squinting against the lowering sun, I keep my eyes trained on the spot where he has entered the stand of trees, and I retrieve my own knife out of the holder in my boot.

A hiss of steel against leather behind me is proof that both of my bondmates have drawn their own swords. Egan is urging his horse slowly forward, gaining ground at a quiet pace.

"Move closer, Murphy." There's no need to whisper as my sore throat causes my words to come out low and raspy.

"Not yet, Love. I know you can handle yourself, but let's watch their backs from a distance." Murphy gives my thigh a reassuring pat.

"It's alright, come closer." Egan sheaths his sword and yells back at us at the same time that I see Cathmor emerge from on his left.

The other man has also put away his weapon and his left hand is holding... the reins of a riderless horse. A familiar horse.

Slotting my knife back in my boot, I urge Murphy. "That's Ciaran's mount. Let's go."

With a slight kick, Murphy urges our horse forward, and we approach Egan and Cathmor midconversation.

"... just wandering. There's no sign of Ciaran or anyone else." Cathmor turns towards us as we near, then drags me off Murphy's lap. "Recognize the horse, Daisy?"

"It's Ciaran's. That's his saddle." Not only his saddle, but his bulging saddlebags are affixed as well. I scour the ground for any sign of struggle, but wherever Ciaran and his horse were separated was not in this area. "Check his bags, let's see if we can find some answers."

Egan is already unbuckling one, and I join him. I rub down the horse's nose, before running my hands down his flanks and stopping across from Egan. The silver buckles easily come undone, and I cautiously peer in the leather bag. There are spare shirts, a flask and at the very bottom a small, leatherbound book.

Plucking the book out, a crystal gleams in the fading light, I wave it over my head. "I found something." Swinging the metal latch off, I open it up to find that it's a school book of some sort. The lettering is neat and precise, though fancier than I'm used to reading.

The Power of the Elements is written across the title page. Underneath it is a triangle illustration. A flame, a drop of water, and a leaf form the points with lines connecting them.

"Cathmor, isn't this the drawing at the bottom of Ciaran's note?" I turn the book in my hands, so the page can be seen by the men on the other side of the horse.

Eyeing the page, he pulls the note from his pocket and compares the two. "It is." Gazing over my shoulder, he states, "Sunset is upon us, let's find somewhere to camp. We can inspect the book once we're settled. I don't want to get caught out on the road. I doubt very much that Ciaran abandoned his horse. Mount up, be alert. We'll stop when we find a defensible area to camp for the night."

I adjust the stirrups of Ciaran's horse before I mount, and once astride, I find myself between Murphy and Egan. We ride slower as the sun sheds its last rays across the road. My hand grows sweaty, keeping a tight grip on my knife, and I inspect the shadows intently.

We are traveling through a short pass, and I anticipate we'll stop soon, there is a grassy knoll up and to the right. Onyx reappears as we ease off the road, and he drops something shiny on the ground behind us before landing on a ledge overlooking the knoll.

Murphy wheels around and hops down beside the item. Crouched down and balanced on the balls of his feet, he inspects it without touching. I keep my eyes trained on him as I dismount and watch as he swings his head to the north. He touches his nose, does a swish with his hand, and then tilts his head in the air. I've seen that spell before. He's trying to scent something.

"Mount up!" Murphy calls back at us, then walks away from what he was inspecting to swing onto his own ride. Whatever Onyx dropped has him worried.

Astride our horses again, I shift uncomfortably in my seat. I was looking forward to a rest after this long day. I'm almost adjacent to Murphy when I smell a wet, foul odor. Glancing down, I see a sword covered in a translucent grey slime. At least it looks grey in the dim light of the moon. But I know, in the daylight, it's green.

"Trolls," Both Cathmor and I speak up at the same time.

"Onyx!" Cathmor calls his dragon, and the creature swoops down from his perch, landing gracefully onto the road before us. "Did you see the trolls?" Onyx taps a claw once on the ground. "You just found the sword?" Two taps of his claw.

"We can't continue to travel." I dismount — again — and start leading my horse away from the road. "Trolls are most active at night. They're slow but smart. They also rarely travel by themselves. If you see one troll, there's usually one or two more you can't see." Tying my reins loosely to a branch, I turn to the men who are still astride their horses. "Get down. Our best bet is to defend this area if necessary."

Murphy and Egan give Cathmor a questioning look as if to see if he concurs with my statement. That angers me more than I want to admit. I've made this trip numerous times. I've seen and dealt with numerous hazards along this road.

"How many trolls have you dealt with? Any of you? I've traveled this road many times, and it's not smart to look for trolls." Exasperated, I cross my arms waiting for a response.

Cathmor studies me, then turns to my bondmates. "We have Onyx and magic. I say we move out."

"You know what? If you doubt me, go ahead and keep going. We can take a vote." Against my better judgment, I let my pride speak up, and — of course — the men decide it would be safer to be on the move.

Grumbling, I snatch my reins up.

"Mount up, Daisy," Cathmor demands, reining in beside me.

"No. I'll go with the group, but I'm not letting myself get plucked out of the saddle. You idiots can either go slow or walk with me." Walking forward, I ignore Murphy, Egan, and Onyx.

With a confident stride, I head north and hear the jangle of harnesses as the men pass and ride in front of me. Onyx lumbers along at the rear, whether at Cathmor's behest or by his own choice, I don't know.

The further north we go, the more prevalent the stench of troll becomes. The moon has risen, and I can see streaks and smears along the rocks. Coming to a standstill, self-preservation kicks in.

"We can't keep going. We're walking straight for them. This — ooze — is fresh. They're up there. If we keep going, they'll be on us." I peer around, seeing a cave opening far in front of us. "Right there. I think that's their den. See how messy the entrance is? They may be out hunting now, but I don't think we need to chance getting any closer."

"I say we keep going. You may be used to traveling without magic, but you have us now, Daisy. We'll be fine." Cathmor rides past, taking the lead, a shimmer of a spell flowing around him.

꽃

The first sign that things are going horribly wrong is the outraged roar from Onyx. Spinning around, I see the sparse-haired head of a troll over the dragon's shoulder. One meaty hand stretched around attempting to gouge out Onyx's eyes.

Onyx gives a full body shake while giving a mighty heave of his wings and taking to the skies. The troll hangs on tenaciously, both hands circling the dragon's horns.

One troll has come out, now, to see where the others are. I don't have to wait long.

Time stretches out as I crouch, pulling my sword and assessing the turmoil happening around me. Egan is assisting Cathmor, fighting off a second troll, while Murphy spins around a third, throwing up shields of water between myself and the green slimy monster.

"Distract him for a little while longer, Murphy, then let him at me!" Giving Murphy and the troll my back, I slide my sword back into its scabbard and leap for the cliff looming above me. Scrabbling against loose rock, I stretch for handholds, extending my legs into any toehold I can find. Adrenaline roars through my body, giving my weakened body a boost to climb.

I find a ledge large enough to stand on, once again eyeing the various fights on the road below and the spinning dragon soaring above us.

"We'll be fine, he says. We have magic." I scoff. I bellow down a growly, "Now, Murphy!"

But the stubborn man shakes his head at me, having been knocked off his horse, he's currently throwing balls and vines of water at the troll. All which are repelled by the slime coating the troll's body.

"Hey, you big pile of snot! Over here!" I wave my sword, hoping the glint off the metal will draw the troll's attention.

But Murphy, the big lug, jumps on the troll's back. He can't get a good grip through the slime, and the creature uses that fact to his advantage. As I watch in horror, Murphy's arm is gripped, and the troll flings my bondmate like a rag doll against the cliff side.

My eyes fill with tears as Murphy lays still, blood pouring from a wound in his head. "No!"

Outraged, I squat, pick up a rock, and peg the troll in the forehead. "Come and get me, you slimy bastard!"

The troll shakes his head and raises a palm to his head. Lumbering my way, he stretches his arms to pluck me off my perch.

Bouncing on the balls of my feet, I hold my sword aloft and calculate. I have to time it just right. One breath. Two. Then with a cry, I launch myself, bringing my sword around and through the neck of the troll. Big slimy arms grip my torso, crushing my ribs.

Holding my breath against the stench, I ride the troll down to the ground, using my momentum to force the sword deeper. The creature falls, arms falling off of me, and deep-crimson blood seeps out, covering us both. Rolling away, I gasp, struggling to get air into my starved lungs.

My whole body shakes as I roll to my hands and knees, crawling past the very dead troll to Murphy. "Cathmor! Egan! Get him restrained then cut off his head!"

I trust them to follow my directions as I strip off my ruined sweater, then my tunic. Shivering in just my undershirt, I fold my tunic and carefully lift Murphy's head, needing to staunch the flow of blood.

Tears drop on his face as I check his breathing. Shallow but still alive.

"Murphy, wake up. Please wake up." The adrenaline that has fueled me is leaching out of my body, and I collapse at his side. "Please."

Loud thumps sound around me, but I keep my focus on Murphy. I stroke his face, futilely wiping blood and slime off his cheeks and brow with my sleeve. "Stay with me, Murphy. Please, please."

19

The heavy weight of a cloak drops over me, then strong hands grip my shoulders and attempt to pull me away from Murphy. I fight against the hold until Cathmor appears at my side, rough hands gently holding my hands, "Let go, Daisy. Egan has you. Please. I can help Murphy."

In a daze, I stare blindly at Cathmor. Nodding, I release my hold on my bondmate and allow Egan to drag me away.

"Onyx?" I listlessly turn my head, searching for the dragon.

"He did well. He's . . . disposing . . . of the bodies." If Egan's sour look is any indication, the dragon is having a late dinner.

"Okay." I grit my teeth against the intense tremors wracking my body.

Egan sits on the ground, legs bracketing my body. Snuggling into his chest, I watch as he extends his palms and makes lazy circles in the air. His hands flare with fire for a moment before returning to normal.

I want to ask what spell that was, when Egan's body warms, penetrating the cloak he wrapped me in and seeping into my body. Taking my hands in his, he slowly rubs, warmth spreading across my cold fingers and traveling up my arms.

"You did so great, *Mo Chroí*. I saw that leap you took. You saved

Murphy's life with that act of bravery." Egan's voice is low and comforting in my ear.

Cathmor grunts. "It was stupid. You could have gotten yourself killed. What were you thinking?"

"Really? *That* was stupid?" My vocal cords are shredded, but I put as much disdain as I can into my reply. "What happened to 'We'll be fine, we have magic?' Most spells just slide off trolls. Did you know that? Next time I say we need to *not* confront trolls, listen to me!"

Cathmor ignores me, using his magic to create a plant-based salve that bonds to Murphy's wound. My unconscious bondmate is rolled on his side, facing me; and I will him to open his eyes.

Goddess, please help my bondmate.

"Watch him, I'm going to round up the horses and our weapons. They need to be cleaned. Egan, do you think you can burn off the slime?" Cathmor rises to his full height, tilting his head left and right to stretch out the muscles.

"No." With a shake of my head, I answer before Egan gets a chance. "Spells won't get it off. If you can make some soap, they just need to be washed clean, then we can oil them and buff out any residue that's left."

"Soap?" Cathmor gives me a skeptical look.

"Not everything needs to be solved with magic, Cathmor. Often the *Mundane* way is best."

"Noted." Striding off, Cathmor flexes his hands at his side. While his hands may be sore, I think he's probably stopping himself from wringing my neck. I take a bit of pleasure at getting under his skin.

"You shouldn't poke the bear, Sage." Egan turns me, so my left side is pressed against his chest. "Are you okay? Any new bruises or scratches?"

"My entire body feels like one large bruise. That troll managed to squash my ribs a bit on the way down. But I don't feel any worse than I did. That might change in the morning, but right now, I'm too worried about Murphy to care."

Gazing up at Egan, I notice he has streaks of slime across his cheek, and a cut above his left brow. "Are you and Cathmor okay?

When I looked over, you both seemed to have been able to keep your troll at a distance."

"We are both unscathed. It took a bit of plotting and cooperation, but Cathmor managed to get enough vines around the creature for me to lop off his head." Egan rubs a hand over my shoulder. "Thank you for that direction. Without it, I have no doubt we'd still be fighting."

I want to argue that they should have listened to me. Being the one with the most experience on this road, they should have trusted I knew what I was talking about. But now is not the time. Relaxing into Egan's embrace I continue my watch over Murphy.

We end up camping in the middle of the road. Egan builds a fire, I place the eggs in the hottest section, and Cathmor sets up our tent above where Murphy remains still. At some point, Egan brings in water for us to clean up, and when we're done, we place our slime-covered clothes in the bucket to soak. It's an unspoken agreement that until we know the extent of his injuries, it's best not to wake Murphy.

§

When I wake up, the first thing I notice is that Murphy is gone.

"Murphy!" Sitting up abruptly, I groan and hold an arm to my ribs. I guess that troll squeezed a little tighter than I remember. With a little more caution, I turn and shake Egan's shoulder. "Egan, Murphy's gone."

Propping himself up on his elbows, Egan peruses the inside of the tent. "I think everything is alright. Cathmor's gone, too. They're probably just outside."

"I'm hurt, Daisy." Cathmor bends his head and enters the tent. "You noticed Murphy was gone but didn't even see that I was missing as well." He sets up two skinned and skewered rabbits over the fire. "We went out and caught some meat. We have some bread left, and we can save whatever is left for lunch."

Murphy enters at a slower pace and places two bows against the inside wall of the tent. With a broad smile, I slowly stand and meet him before he's taken three steps.

He gives me a tilted grin then slides his gaze from my face down my body. He's reached my torso when his face suffuses with a blush, and he hurriedly enfolds me in his arms.

"Love! Your shirt . . . it's. . . . I can see. . . . Egan, toss me a blanket." Murphy stumbles over his words as he tries to walk me backward and keep me in his clutches.

Glancing down, my face warms as I remember I'm just in my sheer undershirt, and I just walked across the tent in full view of all the men. I fear my face will look sunburned by the end of this trip from the constant attention from them.

"I, for one, don't mind the view." Cathmor keeps his back to me, though, as he seasons the roasting meat.

Egan hurries forward with a cloak, which I thankfully tie and hold closed. When I turn to thank him, he stops my words with a quick peck. "I didn't expect such a pleasant sight this morning, but I'm not objecting, either. I'm thinking you may have hit your head harder than we thought, Murphy. You don't usually blush at the sight of Sage."

"Feck off, Egan." Murphy stomps to the fire to help with the meal.

Ducking my head, I scurry to my saddlebag and pull out a clean tunic. Changing the subject seems like a wonderful idea, so I ask, "Was there any sign of Ciaran and his accomplice when you were out?"

"There was evidence of a campsite. Though, the embers were cold. There was also troll slime on the ground. I don't know if the trolls found them before or after they settled down, or if they escaped the trolls, and that was just what dripped off Ciaran and his companion." Cathmor stands, grabs a blanket, and herds me into a corner. "Dress back here. The blanket will shield you."

Surprised at his chivalry, I allow myself to be herded. "No peeking."

Cathmor lifts one eyebrow and grins. "No promises." But he holds the blanket high above eye-level.

Egan takes the time to change while I'm occupied, and we are all as fresh and clean as we can be in these conditions, when we sit to break our fast. The dragon eggs glow orange in the bottom of the fire, and I pray the Goddess has been watching over them.

"This has been the most adventurous Samhain I've ever had." Picking at my bread, I shove a chunk in my mouth, swallowing it down with some chamomile and honey tea. "I think when we get on the road, I should double with someone. I need to look through that book and see if I can get an idea of what Ciaran is doing. We know he's going to get to Firehaven before us. I'll feel safer if we at least know what to look out for."

The men agree with me. We pack up, only taking the time for Murphy and Egan to magically wash and dry our clothes. This time, I ride with Egan, sitting sideways, one leg hooked around the saddle horn, so my hands are free to turn pages.

By the time the two low, stone buildings that make up Firehaven come into view, I am no closer to understanding Ciaran's actions than before.

20

Firehaven is really only two buildings, and the lava pools beyond them. One building is magically enhanced to keep food fresh. Master Riordan and I restocked it over the summer, locking it up tight. I'm not worried about if Ciaran managed to get in. The council put so many wards and spells on the building's lock and key, that if he did manage to get in . . . well, he'd have earned it.

Leading the men to the right, we round the second building to the attached stable in back. Despite the many things that we need to attend to, the horses take precedence. Egan rubs the horses down, while Murphy and Cathmor carry supplies in through the back door. I follow with the eggs.

In the kitchen, I lay the carrier on the wooden table and chase after Cathmor. "I need my bag, please. I'm going to change and deal with the eggs. I can't wait any longer."

Passing it over, Cathmor pauses long enough to state, "Don't go without one of us. I'm serious, Daisy. We don't know where Ciaran is or what he has planned, until he's dealt with, we stay together."

Nodding, I dig through my pack, pulling out trousers, vest, apron, and gloves all made of thick leather. Rushing to a room, I yell over my shoulder, "I'm leaving as soon as I'm dressed. Whoever's coming with me be ready."

There are three barks of laughter and a mumbled, 'undressing would work better' that reaches my ears from the first floor. I roll my eyes. Men can make any sentence dirty.

I don my leather pants, canvas shirt with a vest over it, and a leather apron. Stuffing the gloves in my apron pockets, I jog down the stairs and return to the kitchen. "Who's coming with me?" I raise a hand when all three men open their mouths to reply. "No jokes. Just follow." They snap their mouths closed, but can't hide the mirth in their eyes.

Picking up the carrier and a water jug, I find myself being followed by all three men. "I suggest you leave the cloaks behind. You won't need them at the lava pool." Opening the door, I glance left and right for any trouble, waiting for the men.

Once they join me, I cross the street then take the path behind the food storage. The path is somewhat overgrown, but what little grass manages to grow doesn't survive long. I leave the water jug on the ground where the grass peters out. The closer we get to the lava pools, the more barren the land, until we are walking on black sand. We are all covered in sweat, not from exertion but from the heat of the molten lava we're approaching.

After several minutes, I can feel the metal carrier softening and stop to set it down. "It's best if I go alone from here. It's only a couple of yards. You'll be able to see me." I point to the right. "See how the black is bubbling and sparking? That's all I need. Just one spot to lower the eggs."

Squatting, I unlatch the carrier, don my gloves, then gently lift and place an egg in each of my pockets. With a little wave I leave the men, slowly feeling the ground for any softened spots that I do my best to avoid. My boots have leather soles, but despite the charms that have been placed on them, the heat is intense.

Thankful for the reinforced knees of my trousers, I kneel and slowly drop each egg into the lava as close to the surface as I can stand. Too close and I burn myself, too high and the impact shatters the eggs.

I wipe an arm across my forehead, eyes stinging from the sweat dripping into my eyes. Once the last egg is in, I take a deep breath of the hot, dry air and give a little cough. Breathing is difficult with this searing heat. Easing my way back to the men, I pass them, then break out into a jog and beeline for my water jug.

Shaking my gloves off, I rip off my apron then unbutton my vest, until I'm left in a sleeveless canvas shirt. My body is shaking, the tremors causing the cap to slip in my hand.

"I've got it. Hold on, *Mo Chroí*." Egan leaves the jug in my hand but deftly spins the top off.

My stomach clenches, and I take small sips, knowing I dehydrated rapidly. After three sips, I look up to see three concerned men standing before me.

"I'm dehydrated. If we can move closer to Firehaven, I'll cool down. Murphy maybe you could douse me when there's more moisture in the air to draw from?"

"Of course!" His reply is almost drowned out by my small screech as Cathmor sweeps me off my feet.

Cathmor throws out orders as he jogs with me towards the path. "Egan grab her clothes, keep up Murphy . . . let's get her cooled down soon. She's burning up."

I continue to sip at the water, occasionally wiping my face with the water that spills out as Cathmor picks up his pace. He slows to a stop just inside the treeline. Placing his back to a tree, he lowers us both down until I'm sitting on his lap. Murphy immediately swirls two fingers in his palm making a big ball of water. Then he does a wiggle and a flick, and a mist begins to fall over both me and Cathmor.

"What happened back there, Sage?" Egan squats in front of me, forearms on his thighs and his hands dangling between his legs. "Is it normal to dehydrate that fast?"

"No." I pause to take another sip of water. "Usually Master Riordan and I take turns, so no one is in the direct heat for too long. But there was only me. I only have to do that one more time, and it's a lot quicker."

Cathmor tips his head over my shoulder, "What's the next step?"

"In three days, we'll check the pools. The eggs should break apart by then, and the wyrms should be swimming in the lava. We just have to watch them for five weeks as their legs and scales begin to form." Between the mist and the water, I am feeling steadier. "At that point, we draw them out and walk them to the hot springs. They'll continue to grow at a rapid rate from there. Then we return to Lámhach at the Vernal Equinox."

"Well, that certainly gives us time to read Ciaran's book and hunt him down." Murphy gradually lets the water ball dissipate and pulls me into a hug. "Do you think you can eat? Maybe something light?"

"Yes. Light sounds wonderful and maybe a bath, I sweated out so much. I am ready to be out of these leather pants." All eyes zero in on my legs, and if I wasn't already flushed from the heat, my face would be turning red — again. These men get me so flustered.

21

While the men collect food from the storage building I continue to drink from my water jug. I love this house. It's where I spend three months out of the year and little by little, Master Riordan and I have filled it with books and games that we enjoy.

The outside may be stone, but the inside has a wood interior. The furniture is overstuffed, and I've spent many a winter making rag rugs for the floor and painted pictures for the walls. It has three bedrooms, an indoor bathroom, and one big room downstairs that combines the kitchen and living room.

I'm halfway through my water when the men return. Murphy and Cathmor with their light hair and eyes make Egan with his raven hair and deep-amber eyes appear small. But all of them are over six feet tall and make me feel tiny at a little bit over five feet.

None of them let me help, which is a good thing considering how weak I still feel. Instead, I sit with my back against the armrest of the couch and stretch my legs out. In this position, I can see them making tea, cutting up vegetables, and Egan is heating up some sort of meat.

Cathmor serves up the food and brings two plates with him as he saunters into the living area of the great room. "Sit up, Daisy." He nudges me with a hip, forcing me forward. Settling behind me, he reaches around and hands me a large salad, liberally topped with beef strips.

I balance my plate on my lap, so Egan can hand me a mug of tea. The aroma of chamomile, rose hips, and honey wafts on the steam. Egan takes an armchair across from the couch before saying, "The tea should keep you hydrated. I made a large kettle full, so there will be more after you bathe."

"Thank you, guys, this looks like a wonderful meal." I smile at each of the men, then pose a question to Murphy as he sits in the last available chair.

"Murphy, how are you feeling? Has Cathmor checked on your wound this afternoon?"

"I have a bit of a residual headache, but the healing spell Cath wove did its job. A bit of a scab, and I'll have a scar, but no worries." He gives me a wink, "Next time I'll listen to you when we're in trouble."

"Maybe not always, but while we're here, where I'm used to the dangers that could befall us, definitely." I smile down at my meal, pleased that he's taking me seriously.

The rest of the meal is full of stories about dragons and the types that I've seen, both up close like the blacks, or from afar like the reds and once a silver dragon glinting in the distance.

The meal makes me drowsy, but I still need to bathe. "I'm going to head upstairs. I'd like to wash the sweat and dirt of the day away. And the slime! Ugh, I think it sunk into my pores in places, because I swear I can still smell it."

Cathmor gathers my dishes, and Murphy is quickly at my side to help me rise from where I've sunk into the comfort of the couch. Once I'm steady on my feet, he releases his hold then takes his own dishes to the kitchen.

Hesitantly, Egan approaches me as I'm slowly rounding the couch. "*Mo Chroí*, I'd like to help you if you will allow it? I'd like to tend to your bruises and check to make sure that your ribs aren't broken."

So much has happened in such a short amount of time, and I've not really allowed myself to think about it all. I do have aches and pains that are shouting at me now that I'm not feeling the pressure to get the eggs into the lava pool.

"Do you have healing powers like Cathmor?" Gripping tight to the stair rail, I take a timid step forward.

Egan rushes to place an arm around my waist to support me as I climb to the second floor. "Not as such. It's minor, but I have an arnica salve that will be helpful for the bruises and the pain."

Nodding, I keep my focus on each step, doing my best not to jar my body.

"Egan," Cathmor's raised voice follows us. "Now's the time."

Tipping my head, I spare a glance to the dark-haired man beside me. "The time for what?"

"It's nothing . . . really, let's get upstairs shall we?"

The snickers from the kitchen tell me it is indeed 'something,' but I don't have the energy to pursue it. Luckily, I took the first room to the right and eagerly turn in to get a towel and fresh clothes.

"I'll get the salve and some bandages as well, in case we need to bind your ribs. When you're done with your bath, I'll be waiting here for you. If that's alright?" Egan's cheeks look a little pink. I wasn't sure that his tanned skin *could* blush, but it appears he can.

Smiling at him reassuringly, I place a hand lightly on his forearm, "That's fine, Egan. Thank you."

Once in the bathroom, I turn on the water. It, too, has been magically enhanced, and the water that feeds the hot springs comes spraying out from a bar above my head. I'm thankful for the cedar planking in here. Not only do I have a hot shower, but the steam build up adds to the soothing feeling.

Not sure how long I can stand on my own, I sit cross-legged under the spray to bathe. My hair takes the longest because raising my arms above my shoulders has me gritting my teeth in pain. When I rinse off there is a diluted stream of troll slime, ash, and dirt swirling down the hole in the corner.

I know Egan needs to have access to my wounds, so I slip on a pair of green-cotton leggings and a matching cotton tunic with ties at the side. I leave off my undershirt to allow easy access for Egan to see my ribs.

Padding across the hall in my favorite green-and-blue-striped socks, I spot Egan placing a mug of tea and a water glass beside my bed. He turns when I drop my filthy clothes on the floor outside my door.

"Feel better?" Egan steps to the side to allow me to sit on the bed.

"Much, being clean has helped a bit all on its own."

There's a moment of awkward silence before Egan turns a wooden bowl in his hand. With a slight cough, he speaks. "I need . . . it would be best . . ." Taking a big breath, he starts again, "It's best if you take off your clothes. You can use a towel to cover your . . ." He stumbles over his words before rushing to his room.

Before I can call him back, he returns with a clean towel. Handing it to me, he backs out of the room and pulls the door closed. From the hall he calls, "Just let me know when you're ready."

My entire body heats as a blush travels from my head down my torso as I undress. Laying facedown on the bed, I do my best to cover my bottom with the towel. "I'm ready, Egan."

The door slowly swings open, and I turn my head away, still embarrassed to be naked in front of my bondmate. I'm not sure why. I've done midnight rituals all my life, skyclad, as my mother would say.

"Oh, *Mo Chroí*." Egan's voice breaks as he runs a soft hand down my back.

"Is it very bad?"

"Well . . . at least you look good in purple?" I think this is his way to lessen the severity of the bruising on my back, and I give a little laugh.

"It looks worse than it feels. I don't feel *great*, but I honestly don't think my ribs are broken. I'm breathing okay, and there are no sharp pains."

"I didn't think so." Egan's hand retreats, and when it returns the piney-sage aroma of the arnica reaches my nose. "I'll be gentle, but you're bruised from your shoulders to your ankles. Try to relax."

Folding my arms under my head, I try to ease the tension that's still present in my back and close my eyes. Egan starts at my legs, making tiny circles with his fingers as he spreads the warm salve on the small scratches and larger bruises, decorating my skin. Each pass of his hand is soothing, and my muscles slowly unclench and ease as the pain lessens. He must be using a healing touch, because I've never had this result with arnica before.

He gives one last pass across my shoulder blades before asking me to turn over in a raspy voice. In my tranquil state, I turn over, my body bare to Egan's gaze. His eyes blaze orange for a moment, and his heated gaze slowly peruses my breasts, my stomach, skipping over the towel to my thighs. His eyes stall at the towel on the way back before sweeping up to my face. "Tis a shame such beauty was harmed. Though, the bruising is not as encompassing as it is on your back. The arnica should be able to ease all of this."

Gathering himself, he adjusts his pants, and I smile inside that I have this effect on such a good man. My body tingles thinking about it, and he hasn't even begun to administer the salve on my front yet.

Egan again starts at my legs, making quick work, only slowing down at my thighs. He then lifts the towel to expose my hips, adding a layer of salve on each, gripping tightly for just a minute before shaking his head and focusing on my ribs,

His circles are larger as he treats each purple splotch before laying a hand flat on each spot, heat radiating out. In a quiet voice, he affirms what I already suspected, "Your ribs feel fine. You got very lucky, *Mo Chroí.*"

He runs his hands along the side of my breasts before applying salve to my shoulder then down each arm. When he reaches my left hand, he holds it in his momentarily before bringing it to his lips and placing a soft kiss on my knuckles. "Your hands are so dainty, yet tremendously strong."

My heart stutters at the raw emotion in his voice. It's awe and desire and something *more*.

Raising his head he stares into my eyes, then lowers his head to mine. I'm expecting a soft kiss, such as he laid on my hand. But this kiss is firm and hard and demanding.

Licking at the seam of my mouth, he coaxes my lips open and sweeps his tongue across mine. He alternates between devouring my mouth and sucking my lip into the warmth of his.

My senses are reeling, and I grip his shoulders, feeling as though I'm falling even though I'm reclined on my bed. I meet each thrust of his tongue with one of mine, gasping when his calloused hand encircles my breast, pinching at my nipple.

"Sage." My name on his lips is low and raspy. Abruptly, he stands and holds his hands up. With a quick wave there's a flash of flame across his hands that he smothers by clapping his hands together. "Just cleaning my hands, *Mo Chroí*."

Kicking off his boots, he climbs into bed beside me and rolls me to my side, thrusting a leg between mine before continuing the onslaught on my mouth. He has one arm wedged under my neck, and the other is touching me . . . everywhere. He rubs light circles on my back, then drags his hand down my hip and thigh before reversing and sliding up my side to caress my breast.

My own hands are exploring Egan over his clothes, and as our desire rises, I become desperate in my movements. I shove his shirt up, and he shucks it off as I work at the ties of his trousers.

Cradling my head in both of his hands, Egan asks between drugging kisses, "Sage, are you sure? I don't . . . I don't want to hurt you."

"Yes, Egan, yes, please."

Egan pushes his pants off and kicks them to the floor. Rolling us, he settles me, so I'm astride him. His manhood long and thick before me, a bead of precum glistening on the engorged head.

"You should take control." His pants match mine as I stare down at the gorgeous man that lays beneath me. "At your pace, *Mo Chroí*."

Nodding breathlessly, I stroke him and rise up on my knees. I'm wet and ready for him as I position myself above him. Easing him into my core, I slowly edge down, Egan's hands gripping tightly on my hips. Placing my hands on his forearms, I slide down until he's fully seated inside me.

I close my eyes and try to steady my breathing. "You're so big, Egan. I was scared for a moment you wouldn't fit."

I feel him jerk inside me as he gives a bark of laughter. "You're mine, Sage, the Goddess gave us to each other, we will always fit together."

Nodding, I lean forward and place my hands on his chest, flicking his nipples and enjoying the small jerks his hips give in response. Then I rock forward and back, rising and falling over him at a steady pace.

Egan's moans match mine as his hands roam over my stomach, up to my breasts. As my rhythm quickens, he starts thrusting up with his hips, and I feel a tightening low in my stomach, my climax building. I can only hold on as my body buzzes, and every touch Egan places on my sensitive skin only brings me closer to the edge.

Suddenly, Egan sits up, holding my body securely with his hands along my back as he takes my breast in his mouth.

"Egan!" I scream as my climax washes over me, and with two more thrusts Egan joins me with a roar.

My body drops onto Egan's sweat-coated one, chest heaving and feeling warm all over. "That was—"

Anything I was about to say is lost when Murphy bursts through the door, water spraying out of both palms. "Fire! Goddess! You set the room on fire!"

22

Wide-eyed I stare at the flames licking up the walls, scorching the ceiling and inching their way to the curtains. *Goddess, did Egan lose that much control?*

The man in question shields my body with a sheet and sits me on the edge of the bed. He then raises his hands above his head and whispers a chant before lowering his arms and spinning.

The flames lower and gutter out by the time he's back to his original position. Panting from the exertion, Egan bows his head, hands on his hips.

The room is now wet and smoky. Wrapping the sheet more securely around my torso, I flip the latch and push the window up. A cool breeze floats into the room, and I plop onto the end of the bed before inspecting my sodden room.

The line of the fire is evident on the walls. Two feet off the floor, just at the level of the bed, is a black, charred line that runs the perimeter of the room. The fire didn't start at one spot. It looks like it flashed out from the bed and started a ring of fire on the walls.

"Egan? What happened?" I turn my attention from the walls to the men in the center of my room who are suspiciously quiet.

Murphy and Egan are staring at me. No. Not at me, at my arm.

Looking down, I'm shocked to see my flame tattoo has spread, and now, the mark runs from the top of my wrist around and up my arm to my elbow.

"What?" Laying my right hand along the flames on my left arm, I can feel the warmth radiating off of them.

"I think we completed our binding, Mo Chroí." Egan sits beside me and runs a finger up my arm. I blink. The flames — flicker — where our skin meets. "Sage, will you try something for me?"

Speechless, I raise my eyes to his and nod.

"Think of a flame and snap your fingers." Egan demonstrates, and a small flame dances across the tips of his fingers.

My heart begins to pound as I lift my hand up and concentrate. Half of my thoughts are that this isn't going to work. But deep down, where I've buried all my dreams of being normal, a spark of hope flares to light.

Giving Egan's hand one last look, I focus my concentration on an image of a flame and snap my fingers. There's a quick spark, like flint striking chert, but no flame.

"It's all about intent and will. Try again, Mo Chroí." I digest Egan's words.

Repeating to myself 'intent and will,' I reach deep for that spark of hope, and I snap my fingers again.

A flame!

I made a flame! Me. A Mundane. I did it.

"I did it," I shakily murmur. Hypnotized by the flame, still flickering on my fingertips, I only become aware of my tears when a large hand gently wipes them from my cheek.

"You did it, Love. You have magic." Murphy pulls me into an embrace as I awkwardly hold my flame-filled hand out to the side.

Smiling through my tears, I whisper against Murphy's chest. "I'm normal. I'm a Witch."

"You've always been a Witch, Love. Even when you struggled as a child, you did everything perfectly."

Tucking my fingers into my palm, the flame recedes. "I was a powerless Witch, Murphy. I was so sure, if I just tried harder the magic would come."

"But is it the power that makes us a Witch or a Warlock? You know some are stronger than others. Remember Ross? I think the only thing he can do is move things, small things, from place to place." Running his hand through my tangled hair, he murmurs, "Powers or no, you're perfect for me. For us."

After Egan has me conjure and dissipate a flame several more times, he tells me the fire in the room was my doing. Apprehensive, I inspect the damage again. At the moment of our final bonding, when the magic flared to life, it literally flared out from my body and set the room ablaze.

Cathmor arrives in a stampede of steps and rushes up to my doorway yelling, "I smell something burni—" Startled, he skids into the room, "What happened in here?"

With a small laugh, I shake my head. "I'll let Egan explain. Murphy, do you have some clothes I can wear until we can get this cleaned up?"

Murphy stands with me and leads me out of the room with a hand at my back. "My clothes will all be too big, Love, but we'll see what we can do."

Crossing the hall, I enter the room that Murphy and Egan have claimed. Murphy walks to his bags and pulls out neatly folded trousers, shirts, then tunics. From the very bottom he tosses me a pair of brais, then places a white shirt and blue tunic on the bed.

"I'll wait outside the door, come out when you're ready."

"No, trousers?" I stare longingly at the neat pile he's placed on the desk.

"Not until we can fix the waist, they'll just fall off." he closes the door with a quiet snick.

I drop the sheet and pull the shirt on first. It stops at my knees, and I deftly do all the lacings at the throat. Even fully closed, the collar still droops low. The brais are huge, but I pull the laces tight, wrapping them around my waist to secure them. Last I shrug into the tunic.

"Murphy, do you have any twine?"

"Can I come in?"

"Yes, I'm dressed."

Murphy stops at the open doorway and stares at my legs. "I've not seen your bare legs since we were babes playing in Rosemary's gardens." Raising his eyes, he scans up my body and laughs when he sees how I'm swimming in his tunic.

Spreading my arms wide, I show him how the sleeves surpass my hands. "Can you help me fold the sleeves back please?"

Stepping to another bag, Murphy pulls out a ball of twine then advances on me. Tucking his hands into the unbound sides of the tunic, he reaches behind my back, grabs the end of the twine, then brings both hands forward. He maneuvers it around my waist, looping it two times.

"Hold the ends, Love." Once I have the twine in my hands, he pulls a knife from its sheath by his waist and swiftly makes a cut.

My clothes may look funny, the front of the tunic belted around my waist and the back hanging freely like a shortened cloak, but it is no longer in danger of falling off. Murphy rolls my sleeves, and no matter how unconventional I look, I am glad to be clothed again.

A knock on the wall heralds the approach of Cathmor.

The gruff man gives a bark of laughter when he spots me. "You remind me of a child playing in her elder's clothes." Entering fully, he takes my hand and urges me to spin. "Though I'll not complain about the bare legs. Show me this flame you have."

Eager to show off my magic — *my magic* — I concentrate then snap my fingers. Just like last time, a flame sparks to life above my fingertips. Cathmor holds my arm at my wrist and inspects.

"Congratulations, Witch Sage."

Beaming, I tuck my fingertips into the palm of my hand, and the flames dissipate. "Thank you. Where's Egan?"

"He's drying out your clothes and bedding. I thought we should gather downstairs and go through the Elemental book." He glances between me and Murphy. "You two know him best. Is there any reason to believe he might be bespelled?"

Furrowing my brow, I think about the Ciaran who first asked me out and the man of the last week. Folding my arms across my chest, I play with my rolled sleeves. "He was different when I came back last spring. It wasn't anything alarming. He just started mentioning that he wanted a dragon. He became increasingly insistent. And, well . . ." I look at Murphy, "then he cast the spell on the Midding Gate. He seemed desperate."

"Aye, and desperate men oft turn into dangerous men." Murphy offers this bit of wisdom then places a hand on my back and urges me out of the room. "Let's go read. Best we be prepared."

23

The next three days are spent reading the book, cleaning my room — which still smells of smoke — and practicing my fire magic. The book has yet to yield any information about where Ciaran could be hiding out, so the men take the precaution of setting wards around the house, the storage, and the path to the lava pools.

Egan and I find that not only can I call small flames into being, I can also manipulate already burning fires on a small scale. I not only can feel his emotions, but I can sense where he is. If I'm upstairs I can tell which room he is in. If he's outside, I know which direction he is in.

On the third day, I pack a basket with strips of meat and change into my restored leathers. Murphy grabs the water jug, and Cathmor makes sure his vines are in his pocket. They are worried, and rightfully so, that I might become dehydrated again and are trying to take precautions. Egan also has a plan to practice with the others on controlling the lava, to see if together, they might be able to make the environment safer for me.

For myself, I've been praying to the Goddess that the eggs hatched. No matter what Ciaran has planned, or the new magic I have, my job still remains to take care of the dragons. Leading the way to the pools, I tease the men as we go.

"I thought I was being courted. Doesn't that involve flowers or gifts or something?"

"We're bonded and mated, *Mo Chroí*. But I shall do my best to court you still." Egan's declaration is a whisper in my ear and brings a small tilt to my lips.

"I gave you the clothes off my back to wear. Is that not a sign of my courtship?" Murphy's voice rings out from somewhere behind me, and my lips curl higher.

"They weren't off your back, Murph. Pretty sure they were neatly folded extra clothes from your bag."

"Still counts," he retorts.

"And you, Cathmor?" But the man remains silent.

I'm about to turn and demand an answer when I feel a light weight on my head. Reaching up, I place a hand on my hair to find something leafy tickling my palm. Plucking it off, I find a daisy garland hanging from my fingers.

With a huge smile, I spin and run back to the large man. Bouncing up on my toes, I throw my hands around his neck, my basket and the garland banging into his back. Cathmor's mouth tips up on the left side, and he wraps his arms around my back.

"Daisies for my Daisy. Is that what you want?"

"I was just teasing you all, Cathmor, but they're lovely. Thank you."

Cathmor adjusts his grip and then palms the back of my neck. Tipping his head down to mine, he gives me a soft kiss. "Just for now. I'll expect a better kiss once we get back to the house."

As he lets me slide back down his body, I purse my lips. "Perhaps." Giving him a wink, I back away. "I'll think about it." Turning to the side, I carefully hang my garland on a tree branch.

When the men look at me with inquisitive eyes, I explain. "I don't want it to wilt. I'll grab it on the way back."

༄

At the lava pools, I leave the basket by the grass, hold the raw meat in one hand and gingerly make my way to the lava pool. I don't get as close as last time and stare intently at the soft swells of lava. All I need is a glimpse of white. Something to assure me that the wyrms hatched and are swimming in the molten earth.

I've almost given up when I spot a small head, then another poke out of the lava. Relieved, I toss the meat at the edge as the wyrms swim closer. The two have just grasped the meat when a third head pops up. They all hatched.

Each wyrm is about the size of my hand. Maybe just a little smaller. They already have the distinct shape of a dragon head and spinal bumps along their backs. No sign of scales yet, but it's early days. They still have four weeks to grow their legs and the stumps that will eventually become their wings. Once those show up, I'll know it's time to move to the hot springs.

I finish feeding the wyrms and return to the grass for some water. The men are sitting and conversing. Apparently, they were unsuccessful at manipulating the lava. I sip at the water, Murphy drawing water sparingly from the jug to form a light mist.

"We can't get a firm grasp on the lava. It's earth and fire and something else. It slips like oil from water. The magic is almost repelled." Egan gestures with his hands as he speaks, almost poking Murphy in the eye.

"Watch the fingers, fireboy." Murphy swats the offending hand away then adds, "There's not enough water in the air for me to help add to the magic, either."

Taking one last drink, I stand up and motion for the men to rise as well, "Let's head back. I need a shower, and I really want to collect my flowers."

The men surround me, Cathmor taking my apron for me, and tying it to his belt. Murphy moves to hold my hand but grimaces when he feels the residue from the meat lingering on my palm.

"Uncap the water again, Love, I'll rinse your hands."

Once the men are satisfied they are ready, we head back, stopping only for Cathmor to resituate the garland on my head.

The trip back is spent discussing the book and anticipating Ciaran's moves. I also go through the list of 'friends' he had. It's only now, I realize that we only socialized with his peers from the school or the members of the council. His parents have passed and he's an only child. In fact, Lennon is the only family he has left.

"Do you suspect Lennon, then?" Murphy asks as we are all standing at the side door taking our boots off.

Padding to the kitchen, I drop the basket on the counter, and turn on the water to scrub my hands. "You worked with him, Murphy. Did you know of any friends he might have?"

Shaking his head, he stands by the stairs, one foot on the first tread. "No. But then we didn't run in the same circles, either. Lennon seems like a sound suspect, though. I'm going to shower. I'll be quick, then you can get in, Love." With a wiggle of his eyebrows, he poses a question. "Unless you'd like to join me?"

Egan's and Cathmor's gazes make my blush deepen. "No. I'll wait for my turn. Thank you, though."

Murphy runs up the stairs and soon the thrum of the shower fills the air.

Egan remains in the kitchen, shooing me out with a soft kiss on my forehead. "I'm going to start dinner."

"Come sit with me, Daisy." Cathmor beckons me from his spot on the couch, and I plop myself beside him.

Carefully, I remove my daisies and lay them on the table beside me. Before I can turn back to Cathmor, he grips my waist and hauls me onto his lap.

"I believe you were thinking of giving me a kiss." He strokes some stray hair away from my face and then cups my cheek.

Gazing into his green eyes, I nod. "Still thinking about it."

"What can I do to help you decide in my favor?"

"Hmmm. Would you take my turn at cooking tomorrow?" I tuck my arm under his and snuggle into his chest,

"I thought you didn't like my cooking?"

"Well, it's not *bad,* but there is such a thing as seasonings, Cathmor. Even a little pepper would help." I start making circles along his chest and stomach. "So, no cooking. Will you wash the dishes tonight? It's my turn."

"Aye. I could do that. It's just a couple of flicks of the wrist." He does a half-hearted flick to demonstrate.

"I suppose that deserves a small kiss then." I tip my head back and place a small one on Cathmor's jaw.

"Oh, Daisy. That will not do at all."

Cathmor tips me back, so my head lays on the armrest before claiming my mouth. There's no other word for it. He nips and sucks at my lips before thrusting his tongue into my mouth and tangling with mine.

His lips wander across my cheek to a spot below my ear, causing goosebumps to appear along my arms. I tangle my fingers in his hair and feel his fingers loosening the laces on my top. Cathmor slips a large hand under the fabric stroking my collarbone and rests his palm on the swell of my breast. His pinky wanders out and tweaks my nipple.

I take a shuddering breath and cover his hand with mine. "Cathmor."

"Daisy?" He rests his forehead against mine with his eyes closed.

"I think that deserves two days of dishwashing duty."

The rumble of his laughter reverberates through my body as Cathmor straightens us. Reluctantly, he sets me back on the couch beside him, giving me one last light kiss. He adjusts himself through his trousers and giving me a hooded look demands, "I'll need the shower next, Daisy. I need a cold one."

24

The next two weeks are busy. Cathmor spends time with Onyx, flying around the area searching for any sign of Ciaran and his uncle or any companion. But he comes back with no news each time. The mountain range is vast, and there are many cave systems and areas that are too small for the dragon to get close to.

Murphy takes me on a 'courting picnic' as he calls it to the hot springs. The basket he packs is full of fresh berries, meat strips, and a bottle of elderberry wine.

We talk and kiss. Long, slow, drugging kisses. When Murphy lays me back on the blanket, his large body between my thighs, it's exciting and romantic . . . and natural.

When Murphy slowly pulls my shirt off, there's no blushing as he gazes down at me. I want this. I want him.

His work-roughened hands cause tingles to run up and down my body as he lovingly strokes my face, my shoulders, and my breasts. His long fingers explore my folds with a gentle touch, all the while capturing my mouth in heart-melting kisses.

He enters me slowly, his thrusts slow and steady. He teases me until we're both gasping for breath, our sweat-slickened bodies sliding against each other.

Our climax causes my vision to grey and through my joy, my only thought is — *I'm home*. When I regain my senses, Murphy is laughing beside me a hand held up to the rain pouring down.

"Well done, Love. You made it rain."

When we return, my leg has a full double-wave tattoo that spans my calf and shin to my knee.

❦

"Did she gain your water powers as well?" Egan inquires as he squats and inspects my newest mark.

"I'll say this. I'm glad we were mated, because a very cold rain began falling on us." Murphy laughs at the memory.

I slap his stomach with the back of my hand, then turn it up and make a small circle on the palm. Slowly, a small puddle of water forms, that I promptly dump in Murphy's lap.

Leaning back into the couch cushions, I laugh. But I quickly lose my smile when Cathmor stands and stomps out of the house. With a sigh, I move to follow him, but Egan puts a restraining hand on my knee.

"Let him brood for a moment, *Mo Chroí*. You've yet to bond with him. This has to sting."

Nodding, I relax against Murphy and contemplate what to do about Cathmor. I do have feelings for him, and we've shared many kisses. Yet, he hasn't formally asked to bond with me; I don't know how we go about it.

Bonding with Egan and Murphy happened — not accidentally — but without either of us asking to be bound. The Goddess chose. Now I feel bad about denying the binding with Cathmor not once, but twice.

❦

We've been feeding the wyrms for two weeks, and I'm worried. They've developed their limbs and are now crawling forward for their meals. They even have the beginnings of their wings. But their scales are odd. By this point they are usually grey or black unless they are orange from the heat radiating from the lava. These scales have more of a rainbow hue. Constantly changing, no matter if they are in the lava or not.

Most troubling is their size. They are stunted. They haven't grown much past the size of my hand. I blame the irregularity of the heat the eggs were exposed to on our journey to Firehaven.

I haven't voiced my concern to the men, but I know with only two more weeks to Winter Solstice, I'll have to say something soon. Resolved to speak to them, I throw the last of the meat to the wyrms.

Only Cathmor is with me today. The feedings have become routine, and it is decided all three men don't need to accompany me each time.

I'm walking to him and watching him rise from the ground when I feel arms around me. Arms I can't see. I scream as I kick my legs back.

"Cathmor!"

"Daisy!" Cathmor takes a step towards me. That's all he gets out before he rocks back as though he's been hit and crumples to the ground.

Heart thundering in my chest, I demand weakly, "Ciaran? Are you doing this?" Who else could it be?

There's no answer, but I'm being dragged forward, and a cloth appears out of thin air in front of my face. Invisible hands shove it in my mouth. I feel a hand on my head, hear a murmur of words, and then my world goes dark.

"Look at her arm and leg. She's been bonded twice. Do you think a third will take?" The hushed whisper infiltrates my foggy mind.

"You must try. Without the bonding, we have no hope of bonding with the elementals." A second voice doesn't bother to whisper, but I'm so dazed I can't concentrate to know if it's someone I know or not.

"We haven't even found the eggs. Or any eggs for that matter." There. That voice is definitely Ciaran.

"Just do the binding spell when she wakes. We are running out of time. We cannot go back without them. Her men will come looking soon." The voice is retreating as he speaks, and I get the impression that I'm being left alone with Ciaran.

My hand is lifted and something rough is wound around my wrist. "Bind and stay. So mote it be." It's a familiar spell, but there is no overwhelming urge on my part to complete it.

Ciaran then recites:

> Heart to heart
> Life to life
> We join together
> To share all strife
> Never undone
> Bound as one
> So mote it be.

"Goddess, why is it not working?" Ciaran stomps around a bit and then bends close to me. I can feel his breath across my face. "I know you're awake, Sage. Get up." Ciaran roughly pulls on my arm, and my eyes pop open. Disoriented, I stumble and fall against my ex-boyfriend as I try to get my feet beneath me.

"Why is this so important to you, Ciaran? Why me?"

"We need the dragons, Sage. It's all about politics, power, and needing a change from the old ways." I look in dismay at my surroundings as Ciaran speaks.

We're in a cave. Candles are glowing on the floor, flickering in the slight draft coming from the opening. The walls are slightly damp, and we weave through black stalagmites on our way to the entrance.

Ciaran has tied my wrist with a length of rope and holds the end in his hand. "Come, Sage. Where is the best place to find eggs?"

"I don't know." As if I would tell him even if I *did* know.

"You're a dragon tender. Surely, you know where eggs can be found. Don't lie to me." Yanking me out of the cave, he leads us to the left along a barely-there path. Looking down, I can vaguely see the valley floor, though the volcano across the way is very clear.

"We don't hunt for eggs, we take the ones the mating pair have laid.

It is in the accord that the dragons allow us the eggs. I honestly don't know where to look."

The determination on Ciaran's face scares me. Focusing on taking one step at a time, I dare not look to the right. One misstep, and I'll careen off the mountain side, hitting rocks and trees on the way down.

I search for the small bundle tucked in the corner of my mind that is Egan and Murphy. I can sense them far to the east of where I am. Too far. I hope that they can sense me and find me through our bond.

The path we are on zig-zags, and after ten minutes, we stop on a ledge where Ciaran's uncle Lennon is casting a spell. I feel a weight settle in the air around us.

"What did he do? What was that?"

Lennon sneers at me, "A cloaking spell, Mundane. I'm not surprised a powerless Witch doesn't recognize the magic." Turning to his nephew he asks, "Is she bound?"

"No. She also had no information about where the eggs might be."

Setting out on the path again, Lennon states over his shoulder, "Keep trying. Meanwhile, I say we try closer to the volcano this time."

"We can't!" Horrified, I pull against the rope, attempting to stop Ciaran's forward motion. "We'll die. The heat and fumes are toxic."

"Leave that to me, girl. I have more power than you've ever dreamed of having."

Pleading with Ciaran now, I jog until I'm by his side. "Truly, we'll die. The lava is resistant to magic. Do you think the volcano would be any less so? Please, Ciaran. Listen to me."

The stubborn man just shakes his head, repeating his binding spell over and over. I know I could burn through the rope. But I can only make a small flame, and I'm sure Lennon would spell something stronger if I'm caught.

I don't want them to know that I can do any magic. So, unless an opportune time arises, I'm just going to follow along.

Two days pass, always traveling closer to the volcano. I can sense my bondmates are closer, and once I thought I saw Onyx flying overhead. Lennon, however, is quick with his spells, and when I try to scream, I find myself mute.

As we travel, Lennon sends Ciaran climbing boulders and up to ledges looking for eggs. I could have told them they were wasting their time. But every delay gives my men time to catch up. Every night as we lay down, I can feel them closer.

On the fourth day, we camp early, in a large flat area, covered in black sand. Lennon resets the cloaking spell, and places wards around our bedrolls. When we lay down for the night, I stare at the volcano and the lava steadily flowing out of the top. The sea is close, the salty air mixes with the hints of sulfur, and I can't wait any longer.

My mates are close, if I can free myself, perhaps they'll feel me growing closer and meet me halfway. I have no choice but to try.

I turn towards the south, where I sense Egan and Murphy, and watch as the moon slowly rises. Ciaran's deep breathing indicates he's the first asleep, but he's not the one I'm scared of. Keeping my own breathing steady, despite the rapid beat of my heart, I wait. The moon reaches its zenith and starts to wane before I hear the deep steady breathing of Lennon's slumber.

With shaky hands, I attempt to snap my fingers. I have to physically lean into my bicep and hold my wrist to be steady enough to snap.

A flame sparks to life, and I hold it to the rope around my wrist. Because of the binding spell Ciaran used, the rope does not catch fire. But the flame does snap one strand at a time in a slow pace. Too slow. I weep as the fire begins to singe at the skin, irritating then burning it. By the time the last strand is snapped, blisters have formed on the side of my wrist. But I'm free.

Stealthily, I rise from my bedroll, boots in hand and pad across the gritty sand, heading due south. I've covered several yards, when a buzzing runs across my body, and I'm halted midstep. Panting for breath, I will myself not to panic.

"It's not that easy to get away, girl." Lennon's voice is right beside me, and I look to the side to see him there with a new length of rope. Quickly retying it around my wrist, I cry out as the binding bursts the blisters. "You must really be eager to get away to hold your hand over a flame for so long. Surely, the thought of Ciaran as a mate is not that distasteful. You should be thankful any Warlock wants a Mundane like you."

Biting my lips against the pain, I look away, refusing to engage with this man. I'm not sure what flame he thought I used, but the way he's been so condescending towards me, I doubt he suspects I have magic. I hope so, that's a secret I'd like to keep a little longer.

Lennon is power hungry, and is willing to die to get more. There's no other explanation for wanting to go up the volcano.

Lennon yanks me back to the bedrolls, and as we approach, I ignore the reproachful look Ciaran gives me. We must have woken him, because he is sitting up in his bedroll, hair tousled from sleep.

"It's almost morning. We might as well get on our way." Lennon pushes me towards Ciaran and gathers his supplies into his pack.

"Get your boots on, Sage, and roll up your bedding." Ciaran packs his own things, and then ties my bedroll with his on the bottom of his pack. "Let's go. I have a good feeling. Today, we find our eggs."

25

The stench of sulfur burns my nostrils, and my eyes are watering non-stop when Lennon calls the first break. Both he and Ciaran are suffering as I am. The smell is not the only thing affecting us. The heat is rising, and I know soon, the watery eyes will cease as we dehydrate.

Lennon seems to also be tiring quickly. He's been holding the cloaking spell for five days now. He stands before us, weaving as he starts forming circles over our heads. His murmuring spell is raspy and broken, but it works. The smell is bearable now, though the heat remains.

"Try the bonding spell again Ciaran." Lennon's voice is weak, and he takes a moment to sip some water.

Ciaran coughs, then grabs the jug from his uncle, taking a long draught. He passes it to me, and I quickly sip at the water while Ciaran tries the spell, again.

<blockquote>
Heart to heart
Life to life
We join together
</blockquote>

> To share all strife
> Never undone
> Bound as one
> So mote it be.

Instead of speaking, he just shakes his head at his uncle and takes the jug back. After another drink of water, he passes it back to Lennon then trudges on. "I'll try again later."

I know Egan and Murphy are close, but I don't think they can see us. I hope they have a plan. Looking up, I scan the skies for Onyx and Cathmor. Alarmed, I give a shriek, "The red dragons. Lennon. Ciaran. The red dragons are out."

I'm on the verge of a panic attack. I stumble as we continue on, my focus on the dragons above and not the path.

The earth trembles as a loud thump resounds behind us. My vision blurs as my heart races, and I'm terrified to look behind us.

Oh Goddess, please let that be Onyx and not a red dragon. Please.

The dragon behind us bellows, and Ciaran's spine stiffens as he resolutely pulls me forward.

My throat is parched from the heat now, but I try to talk, anyway. What comes out is a whisper, "Ciaran, stop. I don't want to die."

For a moment, I think he hasn't heard me, but he pulls me close and whispers back, "We must be close if a dragon deigns to land near us. I'm sure of it."

I'm going to die on this volcano. I don't want to die. I didn't bond with Cathmor. I didn't tell my mates I love them. No! No, I won't die like this.

Digging deep, I snap my fingers, and fire flares along my palms. I spin and shove my burning hands at Lennon. My fire gutters out, but it was enough. He topples over from fatigue, the heat, and my push. He must have been close to collapse already, because he's barely fallen when the spells he's been holding falters.

In the distance, I see Onyx. Then my gaze is on my mates and Cathmor running towards me. Reaching out, I whisper for them, the heat drying out my mouth and throat. I'm quickly spun around by Ciaran, who drags me to the edge of the path. Lava is flowing a burning-red below, and I'm mesmerized and scared senseless at how close death is.

I cling to Ciaran as I notice his focus is down and to the right of where mine is. Three eggs sitting on a ledge several feet below us have caught his gaze.

"No, Ciaran we can't get closer." I barely get the words out of my scorched throat, the smell of sulfur is overpowering, and I know we have only minutes before we pass out or expire from exposure.

Ciaran shrugs me off, and starts climbing down, the rope of my bound wrist still in his clutches. Alternately panting in fear and coughing against the heat and sulfur combination, my lungs burn, and my chest clenches as my breathing becomes labored.

Dimly, I'm aware of my men calling me, as I unsteadily climb down after Ciaran. I have no choice. If he pulls me down, I'll surely fall in the lava, and I'm too weak to force him back to the path.

Ciaran has reached the eggs and is trying to grab one when a shower of rocks hit me from above. Blearily, I peer up, breathing shallowly, and I think I'm hallucinating. A vine is slithering down the side of the volcano. I mindlessly watch as it curls around my free hand, creeps up my arm, then twines around my torso.

A moan from Ciaran has me glancing his way as the vine raises my arm above my head. Ciaran has released the rope and is struggling to get a hold of an egg. Somewhere in my numb mind, I know there's a reason he can't, but it slips away, exactly like the egg is slipping away from Ciaran.

The vine pulls, and though my vision is spotty, I attempt to look up again, but it makes me dizzy, and I sway.

"Daisy! Hold on!"

"Bind and stay! So Mote it be!"

The vine tightens, and I open my mouth — the words on the tip of my tongue — but I'm fading fast, and no sound is coming out.

Cathmor's faint pleas reach my ears over the buzzing that's filling my head. "Please, Daisy. Complete the binding. Please, love."

No longer able to see, I scream in my head, my last coherent thought.

"Stay and bind! So mote it be!"

As I succumb to the heat and fumes, I feel weightless, and a whisper crosses my mind.

>*Báirseach*.<

26

A mist is falling. I'm in a bed, and a mist is falling over me. As I swim up from the deep dark, I know it's daytime by the brightness reddening the back of my eyelids. Blinking against the water continuously falling on my face, I look to the side to see luscious ferns, ivy, and other large-leaved foliage.

Was I in a bed in a forest?
Was I dead?

Then the memories come flickering to life in my mind. The crazed ambition shining in both Lennon's and Ciaran's eyes. The madness as they drug me across the mountains, across the volcanic sands, and into the hell of sulfur and fire where they were sure they would find the answer to the power they sought.

I recall the burn of each breath, the stench, and the heat. The hypnotic flow of the lava so deathly close, I was sure I was going to die. Tears fill my eyes at the memory of Cathmor trying to lift me out off the side of the volcano, I believe he felt the bonding would strengthen the vine instead of burning away.

I must have died.
>You are not dead, Báirseach.<

A deep, gravelly voice fills my mind. It's scary and big and familiar, as though I *should* know who it belongs to.

Who is this?

>*My Warlock calls me Onyx. But I belong to you now. We all do.*<

I don't understand.

>*You are Báirseach. The Dragon Witch.*<

What does that mean?

>*It is to you that we, the dragons, owe fealty. Because of you, our powerful offspring shall rise. You and the Three shall be the keepers.*<

Which offspring? The eggs I brought to Firehaven?

>*Your bonding changed them, your powers combined have brought forth Edan, Casey, and Moriarity. Your mates have already named them. The first step to their bonding.*<

Whose bonding? I don't understand. Frustrated, trying to make sense of Onyx's words increases the pressure and headache pounding my head.

>*Rest, Báirseach. We'll talk more when you're rested.*<

Closing my eyes again, I sigh. I'm so tired. Then I'll figure out what's going on. Just a rest, that's all I need. Just a little longer.

My right shoulder aches, as does most of my body.

Slowly, tentatively, I open my eyes. I raise my head, but the movement sends a sharp stab of pain radiating up my spine and into my brain.

Looking up, the familiar timber ceiling of the house in Firehaven swims into view. Confused, I side-eye the other side of the room, to see greenery . . . as well as Egan and Murphy. They must have dragged a couch into the room, they are asleep leaning on each other. Murphy has his arm balanced on the armrest, palm up, a ball of water floating above his hand.

Even in his sleep, he is creating a mist. But why?

With a groan, I push up with my elbows. I manage to sit up on the side of the bed, but even that small movement has made me dizzy.

Steps sound in the hall, and my large blond-haired Enforcer enters. He looks exhausted, hair loose around his shoulders and deep-purple smudges under his eyes. He's carrying two bowls in one arm, and a kettle in the other, his attention fixated on not spilling whatever is sloshing in the bowls.

"Hey, Cathmor." I speak softly, my throat is dry, and that's all I'm able to get out, but it's enough to startle the man.

One bowl crashes to the floor, before he regains his equilibrium. He haphazardly places the other bowl and kettle on the table by the bed before rushing to my side, ignoring the broken crockery on the floor.

"Daisy." Cathmor's voice is husky as he kneels before me. He wraps his arms around my waist, burying his head in my lap. "Lass, I am so relieved you're awake."

As I run my hands through his hair, Egan and Murphy wake. The fear on their faces morphs into relief when they see me.

"*Mo Chroí.*"

"Love."

They take seats on either side of me, engulfing me on each side.

"Water?" I croak.

Murphy reaches over to the side and pours some water in an earthen-ware cup. Reaching for it, the sleeve of the shirt I'm wearing slips away from my arm. I hesitantly push my sleeve further up to see a vine tattoo entwined around my wrist.

Letting the fabric fall back, I take the cup and drink. Once my throat is not as dry, I look at the man at my feet. "Cathmor? The bonding worked?"

Sitting back, the large man wipes his eyes with his sleeve and nods. "It did. It-it was close, but the bond took, and . . .," he pauses and looks at the other men before continuing, "and then a red dragon plucked you up and flew you to safety."

I sip more water before speaking. "I think one of you needs to tell me what happened."

Egan opens his mouth, but I hold a hand up. "But first I need to know, what happened with Lennon and Ciaran?"

"Lennon is dead. He expended too much energy on his magic, and in his weakened state, could not withstand the dangers of the volcano." Murphy's voice is filled with anger when he answers. "Ciaran is healing.

We have him bound in your old room. He'll need to answer to the council."

"My hatchlings?" I was dreading that answer. They were stunted when I was taken, and I'm not even sure how long it's been since that point.

Cathmor clears his throat, "We're not sure. You've been unconscious since yesterday. We've taken turns to go to the pools and feed them." He hesitates, "We think, maybe, that they're the elemental dragons from the book."

"What?" Astounded I look at each of my men in turn. "What do you mean?" Then I remember what I thought was a dream. Onyx speaking to me.

"The three hatchlings have grown. They . . ." Cathmor pauses, then stands and heads for the door, "You'll need to see for yourself."

Egan takes Cathmor's place and looks up earnestly. "We knew when you were taken. Murphy and I could feel you moving away from us at a fast clip. We followed but not fast enough. While we could sense your general direction, we couldn't find you." From his downcast eyes and pulled-down lips, it's obvious there is some guilt for being unable to find me.

"Lennon was using a cloaking spell. He only released it if we were camping in a cave." I infuse my explanation with as much comfort as I can. "You can't be to blame for not finding me sooner."

"Blame or no, we almost lost you. We were too slow. My heart stopped when I saw you climbing down towards the lava. If it wasn't for the dragon. . . . I never thought I'd see a red dragon that close. We saw the vines snap back at Cathmor and saw you fall backward." Egan grips my hands tightly. "The dragon swooped in and plucked you and Ciaran up, then left you on the ground by Onyx."

"That explains how I didn't die, but what's all this?" I point to the foliage and mist.

"You were having trouble breathing. Our combined healing only did so much. We had steam in here with Egan's help, and the plants were to freshen the air." Murphy runs an unsteady hand over his hair, "You were . . . you were burned in places, the mist was — is — to help the healing."

Murphy tips me closer into his chest before answering. "As soon as your bonding with Cathmor took, I — we — could feel your pain. It's how we knew how to heal you. We could tell what ails you. Besides the burns and your lungs, your arm was dislocated when Cathmor tried to yank you back up to the path."

"I'm better now. I still ache, but I'm alive thanks to all of you. You said Lennon is dead. How is Ciaran faring?" The angry, petty side of me hopes that he's in pain. But no matter how disillusioned I am with the man, I don't want him dead.

"He's much the same as you. We healed you both the same, but he's bound to his bed." Egan turns at the sound of footsteps on the stairs. "Cathmor is returning."

Cathmor enters the room with small colored bits of *something* in his hands. Approaching me, my newest bondmate extends his hands to me to expose three small dragons. They are perfectly formed, from stubby horns to tails with small finger-sized wings.

"Daisy, meet Edan, Casey, and Moriarity." Cathmor deposits the red, green, and blue dragons on my lap. The red yawns, and a tiny puff of steam floats out of its maw. The green one sits on its haunches staring at me, while the blue one curls around itself before dropping his head on my knee.

"Well, hello, you cute little things." I run my fingers across the tiny dragons, each eight to ten inches long.

A tiny chorus of voices answer in my mind.

>*Hello, Báirseach.*<

27

Cathmor performs another healing spell. I still have some residual aches, but I'm breathing freely, and I no longer cough when I want to speak.

Egan presses the bowl on me, urging me to eat. Between spoonfuls of broth, I disclose the name given to me by the dragons and everything else that Onyx shared with me.

Egan is astounded. Murphy, being so laid back, takes it in stride. Cathmor however, peppers me with questions I don't know the answer to. The why, and how of it all is beyond me.

Edan has been flitting around Egan, while Moriarity lounges on Murphy's shoulder. Casey has been flying around the plants, and they visibly perk up, as she passes.

"Daisy, I no longer feel the bond with Onyx. Do you think he'll be staying here when we leave for Lámhach?" Cathmor's voice is ragged. "I . . . did I do something for him to break the bond?"

Placing my bowl to the side, I reach up and cradle Cathmor's face. "No. He . . . says he belongs to me now. But that you need to bond with Casey."

"Aye, I can feel the power in the little dragon. It is so similar to mine." As he speaks the green dragon alights on his shoulder.

"Edan feels like my fire," Egan adds.

"Little Mori reminds me of the ocean," Murphy offers.

"I think the elementals are meant for you. There's a reason for all this. I think I need to speak with the dragons. I don't know what this all *means*. If you all wish to bond the little ones, I know the bonding spell. Ciaran repeated it so many times, I have it memorized." Remembering that the man in question is nearby, I continue, "Perhaps we need to speak to him about the dragons. He must know more than what was in the book. He and Lennon were desperate to acquire them."

The men nod at me.

Egan speaks up, "Why don't you and Cathmor go outside and speak with Onyx? Murphy and I will check on Ciaran and see what else he knows."

Decided, Edan and Moriarity settle on my shoulders as Egan and Murphy head down the hall. Tired, but eager to be moving, I follow Cathmor downstairs. I deposit my dishes in the sink, and we walk outside where Onyx has been joined by a large red dragon and a slimmer silver dragon.

※

>*Good day, Báirseach.*< Onyx greats me.

>*You are in good health again. I am pleased.*< The red dragon's voice is smoky and smooth.

>*Báirseach.*< The silver speaks in a throaty voice, tipping his massive head down in greeting.

Hands resting on my waist, Cathmor stands behind me, lending me support and comfort.

"You call me Báirseach, Dragon Witch, but what does that mean?" I tip my head back in order to see the slitted eyes of the dragons.

>*You are more than Dragon Master. To you falls the duty of ensuring the lives of all dragons. The younglings have powers we do not. We are leaving them in your and your bondmates' care. They are yours to protect.*< The great red dragon raises a talon, and the three smaller dragons flit over to land on his claw.

>*We formed the accord with the last Báirseach centuries ago.*< The large silver dragon takes up where the red has left off. >*He did not choose his bondmates well. They abused the power. What once was a land of numerous dragon breeds has been whittled down to just three. The blacks, reds, and me. I am sadly the only silver left in existence. The covens suffered as well. The villages beyond the mountains all died out and now there is only the Farriage, Lámhach, and Craobhan covens left. The survival of all relies on the balance of Witches and dragons.*<

I shiver to think what Lennon and Ciaran would have done with extra power. I'm also apprehensive. Though I have use of my bondmates' powers, I have found I do not have normal magical powers. I am still, essentially, a Mundane.

"But what do I *do*? How do I ensure the safety of the dragons, of the covens?" I'm still at a loss to how having these extra powers can help or harm.

"Are they answering you, Daisy? Are you truly conversing with the dragons?" Cathmor's voice holds awe and trepidation.

My 'yes' is accompanied by nods from the three dragons.

>*There are those who come across the sea. Mundane who have forgotten their coven roots. They desire us. They want our horns and scales. Others want to cage us.*< Onyx answers my questions. >*Cathmor, the other Enforcers, and the champions guard the shoreline from invaders. You must speak with them about those who come across the sea. For they are coming, and you must be prepared.*<

"What happened to the last Báirseach? How did he and his mates abuse the power?" I'm curious, but I also need to know what to be careful for, how to avoid the same mistakes.

>*They used the power over their covens. They ruled absolutely, and those who did not bow down to them were put to death. They demanded the best of everything, leaving the rest to the others. But the supplies they allowed their peers to keep were not enough to sustain the covens.*< The silver dragon turns and curls up on the ground before continuing. >*They enslaved my kind to meet their demands when the covens waned. They used their elemental powers to defy nature and force the weather and the growth cycles.*<

>*The result was the death of covens and the silver dragons. Their elementals soon became weary from the use and abuse of the power. When they died, so did*

the Báirseach and his mates.< The red dragon backs up and eyes the door to the house as Egan and Murphy walk out. At their arrival, the small dragons alight on the shoulders of my mates. *>Those who remained, congregated into the three remaining covens that you know now. Learn from the past. Use your powers to aid your covens, keep the borders safe. Help keep our eggs safe, Báirseach, Dragon Master. In doing so, the elementals will thrive and expand your lives. Perhaps in time, they, too, will mate and naturally birth more elementals. They are the hope of dragonkind.<*

"May I know your names?" I can't keep calling them red and silver.

>Our names are not easily said in your tongue. But I have been called Flynn.< The red gives his name with a throaty laugh.

>I've been called Liam.< The silver dragon offers.

"Thank you Flynn, Liam. Thank you Onyx. I will share with my mates your words and concerns." With my words, Flynn gives me a bow and leaps into the air and flies toward the volcano.

>I think I shall stay and help transport you back to Lámhach. Wake me when it is time to travel.< Liam closes his eyes at these words, and Onyx offers a last bit of wisdom.

>Complete your bonding. Only then can your mates bond the dragonlings.<

This has me blushing at the thought of mating with Cathmor. My bondmates curiously look between me and the remaining dragons. Thus far, I know they have only heard my side of the conversation. I'll discuss with them all that the dragons disclosed, but perhaps, they don't need to know why my face has become as red as a tomato.

"Thank you, Onyx. We'll go inside and make plans to depart. Will you be returning with us?"

>You and I will bond when the others do. Then I will return with you.< The large creature ambles off, and I am left with a sleeping silver dragon and my bondmates.

Shaky and a little queasy, I turn to the men. "Let's go inside. I have a lot to tell you, and I'm eager to know what Ciaran has said."

28

The men are quiet as we enter the house. I can feel their eyes on me and their curiosity, but I wait until we are settled in the living room before speaking. Egan and Murphy recline on either end of the couch, while Cathmor pulls me onto his lap in an overstuffed chair.

I relate all that I learned from the dragons, stopping and starting to try to answer questions as I go. It crossed my mind that they might think I'm crazy or hallucinating about speaking with them. But none of them question it. They have quite a few questions about the bonding and the responsibility of being bound to the little ones, but my communicating with the dragons they take in stride.

The dragonlings are full dragons but more playful than their larger counterparts. Edan is at the table, sticking a claw in the flame and transferring it to his other claw, bouncing it around like a ball. Casey is on the armrest of our chair, twirling one of the daisies that Cathmor has made and is busy braiding. Moriarity meanwhile, is splashing in Murphy's cup of water, making and popping bubbles with abandon.

For a moment, we dwell in silence, entertained by the small dragons. Our peace is disturbed by a shout from Ciaran. "Sage! I want to speak to Sage."

"We told him you would come when you were ready. Do you wish to speak with him?" Egan puts a hand out and grabs the fire from Edan before the dragon can set fire to the couch.

"Did he tell you anything?" I take the daisy chain from Cathmor and place it jauntily on his head.

"He said he was a descendent of the last elemental bondmates. Said he and Lennon deserved them. The power was theirs by rights. He broke down after we broke it to him that Lennon died on the side of the volcano." Egan sounds remorseful that he had to be the one to tell Ciaran about his kin.

Taking a deep breath, I rise and glance up the stairwell. "No time like the present. Cathmor, will you come with me? Egan and Murphy, if you could put some provisions together? I think the quicker we return to Lámhach the better. If the council has not taken down Ciaran's ward, the shore is undefended. We've been gone for a month, more than enough time for something to have occurred. I don't like the thought of the covens being vulnerable."

Cathmor places the daisies on my head while taking Casey and depositing her in a potted plant by the door. Then he leads me to the stairs with a hand on my lower back. Tingles run up my spine from his touch, and I can't help but think about the need to complete our bonding. We may need to do it, but more than that, I want to. I can't deny my attraction for the arrogant man.

Once upstairs, we turn into the bedroom on the right, the walls still bearing evidence of the fire I started from my mating with Egan. There are plants in here as well, and a very irate Warlock chained to the bedposts.

"Sage, you must release me. I must find the elemental dragons. I need your help." Ciaran demands, even though he is in no position to ask anything of me.

Though I'm beyond angry at all this man has put me through, there is another emotion overriding it. I pity him and his delusions.

"Ciaran. We will be taking you home to answer to the council. You no longer have the right to demand anything of me. You used me and almost killed us both!" Alright. Maybe my anger is alive and well. "What were you thinking?"

"You are the perfect one to bind with. You have no powers. Once I have the dragons, they will be all mine. I won't have to share their power." Ciaran's face is a mottled red, and spit flies out of his mouth as he rants. "I deserve them! They are my legacy. With them I can control the direction of the school and the council. No one can deny me!"

"Cathmor, he's mad. We need to get him home and turn him over to the council." I whisper, so as not to rile the man on the bed further. "What do we do until then? He's going to hurt himself."

Ciaran is thrashing on the bed, yanking at his restraints. Blood is dripping from wounds on his wrists where the metal is scraping against his skin.

"I'll deal with it. Go back downstairs, Daisy." Cathmor ushers me out to the hallway, taking a right towards his room.

I lean against the wall, heart thundering and wait for Cathmor to return. He doesn't make me wait long as he returns with a small pouch.

"Stay out here, Daisy. I'm just going to put him to sleep." Stepping into the room, Cathmor shakes a powder onto his palm, chanting as he approaches Ciaran. With a soft puff he blows the powder into Ciaran's face, and my ex-boyfriend quickly quiets and falls into a restless sleep.

Tightening the laces on the pouch, Cathmor joins me in the hall, hands behind his back. "I need to wash my hands. I don't want to get any on you."

"I can help with that." Raising my palm, I circle a finger over it the way Murphy taught me. Once there's a flow of water going, I motion to Cathmor. "Put your hand out."

With a smile, he extends his hand, and I slowly pour the water into his palm. Cathmor quickly rubs his hands together, then rubs them down the side of his pants to dry them off.

"Come, Daisy. I'm sure we can help pack up. Then we'll have some dinner." Cathmor snatches up my hand and leads me into his bedroom, where my things have been moved. "Just leave out clothes for tomorrow. The rest we'll take downstairs."

We make quick work of packing, even taking time to move and plant the foliage that Cathmor grew outside.

Dinner is an interesting affair. Edan and Mori trying to 'help' but instead wind up setting the curtains on fire and overflowing the sink. Egan and Murphy are frazzled from cooking and — literally — putting out fires and dealing with overflowing water.

I can hear Liam and Onyx chuckling in my head. Liam speaks up, >*They'll settle down once bonded. Your mates should be able to talk to them just as we can speak with you.*<

The men seem relieved when I pass that on.

"I'll be glad for that. Edan seems to be determined to set the house on fire." Egan holds the little red dragon to the candles and allows Edan to light them.

"You'll notice my Casey is not causing any problems," Cathmor brags, and I can't help but giggle.

He hasn't noticed yet, but one of the vines from Ciaran's room has grown, and Casey has managed to grow it large enough to trail down the stairs and totally encase the railing.

"Aye, Casey's a good dragon." Murphy agrees with Cathmor then points to the stairs. "Perhaps you might check, though, that our prisoner is not lost in a jungle upstairs?"

Spinning around, Cathmor roars, "Casey!" raising his arms he takes control of the growth, and it starts retreating up the stairs. We can hear him mumbling as he works his way to Ciaran's room. "I never had issues like this with Onyx."

By the time Cathmor returns, the dragons are settled in the middle of the table with some food, and our dinner is plated and ready to be eaten.

We discuss our route over dinner, the horses will need to be returned to the stables in Lámhach, so Egan and Murphy have volunteered to ride them home. We'll try to stay in sight of each other, though. Barring any unforeseen dangers, the trip should take two days. We should arrive the day before Winter Solstice.

I'm eager to be home to see my family and pleased that we should be back in time for Rosemary's wedding. I worry about not bringing back three big, black dragons like we usually do. I don't know how that will be received. Nor how well the council will like that the dragons I will be bringing back will already be bound.

Do the council know about the elementals? Do they think it is just a fairytale? What will they think about my new title?

These things and more spin in my head as we head upstairs for the night. We stand in the hallway indecisively as we realize we have two bedrooms and four people.

"Murphy and I will share this room." Egan points at the room where they put me to heal, "You two take Cathmor's room. And as you told me Cathmor, now's the time."

Egan plucks Casey off Cathmor's shoulder and walks into his room. Closing the door he peeks out, "Sleep well, *Mo Chroí.*"

29

Shyly, I follow Cathmor to his room. It looks very stark now that we've packed everything and set it downstairs. I move my clothes for tomorrow off of the end of the bed and place them on the desk by the window alongside Cathmor's pile.

When I turn back, Cathmor is facing the bed and pulling his shirt over his head. Along his upper back is a large marking of a pair of dragon wings. They span from arm to arm in green and black. Without thought, I reach out and trace them with a finger.

Cathmor tenses for a moment before releasing the tension and turning his attention to the laces on his trousers. "The others showed me their marks on their hands and wrists. We figured mine showed up on my back because I braced the vine with my body, trying to haul you up." Turning, he stands before me with his trousers hanging off his hips, the laces dangling freely. "If I'd known the bonding would burn away the vine, I would not have been so insistent. I'm sorry, Daisy. I could have lost you by demanding we bond."

My grey eyes scan Cathmor's green ones, remorse evident in his lowered brow. Stepping close I wind my arms around his waist, I pull him close, laying my head on his chest.

"I tried to break away from Ciaran. I pushed Lennon, and in his weakened state he fell, that's when the spells broke." I tip my head back to look up at Cathmor. "But do you know what drove me? I wanted to live. I wanted to see my bondmates and bond with you. I was so scared the bonding wouldn't take because I was unable to talk when you asked it of me. All I could do was scream it in my head. Because I wanted it with everything in me. I wanted you."

With a groan, Cathmor cradles the back of my head with one hand and my waist with the other, and presses his forehead to mine. "I want you, too, Daisy. So much. Can I have you?"

Nodding, I rise on my toes and press a kiss on his lips. Cathmor returns it, placing small kisses on the corners of my mouth and the tip of my nose. Then he sits back on the bed and pulls me in, so I'm standing between his legs.

With sure hands he unlaces my shirt then gently pulls it over my head. Bare except for my trousers, I feel my blush on the tips of my ears and cheeks. My neck and chest warm as it travels south.

"You're so beautiful." He runs his hands down my neck, across my shoulders, and down my arms. Lifting my hands, he compares my wrist tattoos, one flame and one leafy vine. Placing a kiss on the vine, he slides his lips up. He leaves a kiss on the inside of my elbow, on my shoulder, and at the dip of my collar bones.

A warm, heavy feeling begins below my belly button, and my breathing deepens as I wait to see where he will kiss next.

Raising his hands, he settles my breasts in the v between his thumbs and pointer fingers. Keeping his eyes on mine, he slides his thumbs up and lightly flicks my nipples. He gives a satisfied smile at my gasp, then leans forward to take a nipple in his mouth, licking and sucking before switching his attention to the other one.

When his hands dip into the back of my trousers, my legs go weak, and I cling to his biceps to keep from falling. Gently, he eases them off of my hips, and when they land with a soft whoosh on the floor, he leans back to gaze at me.

I take the time to inspect Cathmor as well; from his defined muscles on his arms and torso to the purple tip of his shaft straining against the loosened laces of his trousers. Unable to resist, I reach down and gently stroke him and am pleased at his sharp inhale.

Cathmor stands so suddenly, I almost fall back, but his reflexes are quick, and he holds me steady by my upper arms. "Easy, I've got you." He shoves his pants down then sits on the edge of the bed again, bringing me with him. "Come here, Daisy."

Grabbing my thighs he lifts and positions me, so I'm straddling him, his cock rubbing my slick core and making my breathing ragged. He's bigger than the others, but he feels wonderful.

Linking my arms around his neck, I rock my hips forward. Cathmor responds with a jerk of his hips before biting at my lower lip, licking away the sting. Aggressively kissing me, I meet each thrust of his tongue with one of my own, rubbing my nipples against his chest.

Cathmor squeezes my ass, then rolls us, so I'm laying on my back looking up at my gorgeous bondmate. "I'll try to be gentle, Daisy, but I need you."

Lowering a hand to my folds, he finds my bundle of nerves that have grown so sensitive, I arch my back at his first touch. He teases me mercilessly. Circling, then pinching, dragging a finger to my opening and spreading the wetness before flicking my clit again.

"Please, Cathmor."

"Please what? Tell me what you want." Cathmor rasps out.

"You . . . I want . . . you. I need . . . you. Please." Panting, I try to make my wishes known.

"Aye, lass, I need you, too."

With a sharp thrust, Cathmor enters me, still playing with my clit.

"Cathmor! Yes!"

He sets a steady pace, and soon, I find myself lifting my hips higher, trying to urge him faster. But he won't be rushed. He pulls out until only his tip is in me then reaches out and pinches my nipples, using his other hand to hold me down. Then he thrusts in again.

Over and over, he does this until finally he relents, after he has me begging for release. Then his movements speed up, and I feel my walls quivering, my stomach muscles are tensed.

With one swivel of his hips, I'm over the edge, back arched, head tipped back and seeing stars behind my eyelids. With one last thrust, Cathmor joins me, and I feel his release as he throbs inside me.

Cathmor collapses to my side, pulling me into his arms.

"I love you, Cathmor."

Placing a kiss on my hair, Cathmor pants out, "Love you, Daisy."

Once we've recovered, Cathmor stands and lifts me off the bed, keeping me in his arms as pulls the covers back. Depositing me in the middle, he slides in, then gathers me close again.

As we snuggle together, I lay my hand on his stomach and notice my mark has grown. Lifting my arm, I show Cathmor.

"Look, the ivy is twining all the way to my elbow now."

Cathmor turns my arm this way and that to inspect it before lowering it and placing my hand on his heart. "You're mine now, Daisy. Completely."

Nodding sleepily, I agree, "Completely."

30

"I'm just commenting. When Sage and I completed our bonding she set the room on fire." This is Egan's excuse for popping his head in the room and inspecting, early the next morning. Eyes bouncing around the empty room, looking for magical evidence of Cathmor's and my final bonding.

Murphy lays his chin on Egan's shoulder, "She made it rain when we went on our picnic, this is almost a disappointment. I was expecting . . . I don't know . . . an explosion of daisies or something."

Wrapping the sheet around myself, I give Cathmor a quick kiss before heading for my clothes. I lift them up and glance out at the window, The sun is just rising, and the purple of the night is giving way to the pinks and oranges of the morning. But that's not what grabs my attention.

Every tree, bush, and plant within view has grown and bloomed. The scrawny brown excuse for grass has thickened, spreading out from the house in an ankle-deep carpet of green. Wildflowers dot the edges, and I'm amazed at the explosion of color, where before, there was wilted plants, brown and drab green.

Skirting around the desk, I shove the window up and peer over the edge of the sill to the ground below. The men are still joking, Cathmor's sleep-roughened voice coming closer. Then I see his two hands bracketing mine, his chest warming my back as he, too, looks out the window.

He wraps his arms around my waist and whisks me away from the opening. Pointing at it, he calls Egan and Murphy. "Maybe take a glance outside before you continue teasing me."

Cathmor spins me in his arms and delivers a knee-weakening kiss. Egan and Murphy are exclaiming in the background as they pound Cathmor on the back.

Smiling at the absurd men, I back away and stick a thumb out, pointing behind me. "I'm going to take a shower." I'm at the turn when I remember our little friends and look over my shoulder, "Where are Edan, Mori, and Casey?"

"Out with Onyx and Liam. I assume they'll be back soon." Murphy brushes by me, planting a kiss on my temple, "I'll start breakfast, Love."

Satisfied that things are going well, I wander to the bathroom, ignoring the outraged rumbles of a now awake Ciaran.

※

Packing our items on one of the horses, Egan and Murphy pull out their cloaks and swing them over their shoulders. I flip mine over my arm and check each room, to make sure nothing is left behind. Through the front windows, I can see Cathmor with Ciaran, the latter bound and sitting as far as possible from the three large dragons, roaming in the yard.

Satisfied that the house is clean, I exit and join my men at the front of the horse.

>*Báirseach, are you ready for the binding?*< Onyx rumbles in my head as he strides to sit beside Flynn and Liam.

"We're ready." Standing in front of the dragons, I take a deep breath and throw my cloak on, leaving my arms free.

Egan, Murphy, and Cathmor stand tall across from me, and then each dips a hand into the inner pocket of their cloaks. Edan, Mori, and Casey emerge and flit up to their shoulders.

Ciaran's eyes shine with greed when they appear. It's disquieting to see, and I'm glad that we are bonding before we leave. I wouldn't put it past Ciaran to attempt to steal one or all of the tiny dragons.

Moving between Onyx's legs I lay my hand on his chest.

"Thank you, Flynn and Liam, for witnessing our bonding." I peek at the red and silver dragons flanking Onyx.

>*We are here to bond, as well. Through the three of us, you will bind all dragons. You are Báirseach.*< Flynn's smoky voice resonates, and my heart speeds up at his words. So much responsibility. >*Do not be afraid. The Goddess knows what she's doing.*<

Shaking my hands out, I put one back on Onyx. "Ready to bond with your dragons?" I ask of my bondmates. They draw closer to me, and Cathmor starts us off.

> Heart to heart
> Life to life
> We join together
> To share all strife
> Never undone
> Bound as one
> So mote it be.

A flash of heat runs along my back and then . . . oh, Goddess. The voices! Grabbing the sides of my head, I fall to my knees. Hundreds of deep voices, thrumming through my head, a cacophony of sound I can't think around. Cowering, I tuck my knees up, trying to help cover my ears even though the sound is coming through my mind.

I'm not sure how long it lasts. At some point, I'm no longer conscious, just *aware*. I'm drifting in a sea of reds and blacks and silvers. Closer? How do I tell distance? There are a small red, a small blue, and a small green, floating closer and closer.

I wake with a gasp, flat on my back, tears streaming down my face. Mori, Casey, and Edan are hovering over me, my men kneeling and staring at me with concern.

"What happened, Love?" Murphy scoots closer to me, lifting me into his lap.

"The bonding . . . the dragons . . . I . . ." Brushing my bangs to the side, I rest my forehead in my hands. "It overwhelmed me. I can hear them. All of them. And they're all here." I point to my head.

"You were screaming. I — we — were scared for you." Egan squeezes my knee before standing. "I'll get you some water."

"Take your time, Daisy. Rest." Cathmor gathers the small dragons, tucking them into his cloak. "When you're ready, we'll get on the road."

Weak and shaky, I lean into Murphy. "I'll be ready soon."

There's a low buzzing in my brain, I know it's the dragons talking, but if I concentrate, I can tune them out. When I feel like I can handle the extra information running through my mind, I tap Murphy's arms at my waist.

"I think I'm good now, Murphy." Together we stand, and I gaze around the yard. Egan walks to me with a jug of water, and Cathmor has the reins of our horses.

"We have a problem," Cathmor announces. "Ciaran took off, either when we were bonding or while we were checking on you. He's still bound, but he's taken a horse with supplies."

Rolling my eyes, I sigh. "He only has two options. Take the road back to Lámhach or remain, bound, in the dragon lands. My guess? We'll catch up to him on the road."

31

Edan and Mori fly around Egan and Murphy when they mount their horses. Casey stays in Cathmor's pocket, a flower popping up every now and then as she plays in the dirt held within. Onyx agrees to carry Cathmor, so I climb onto Liam's back. Leaping into the sky, the dragons give a huge flap of their wings and take us skyward, circling the yard.

Feeling apprehension at the coastline being without dragon protection, we set off at a clip. Lunch is spent at the knoll near where we encountered the trolls almost a month ago. There is still no sign of Ciaran, but if he's smart, he's staying out of sight.

It's close to dinnertime when we spy him. It appears he was knocked off his horse and is laying crumpled on the ground. Ciaran's horse is grazing calmly in a nearby field. Egan and Murphy are crouched beside him when Liam and Onyx land on the road.

Cathmor and I walk closer. I'm limping a little, unused to riding a dragon for so long. By the time we arrive, Egan and Murphy are debating and observing something beside Ciaran.

"It looks like the leather broke."

"You think it was a necklace?"

"Don't touch it."

"Did no one see it when we were healing him?"

Cathmor peers over them then taps their shoulders, "Back away."

"What is it?" I make a move to see for myself, but Cathmor restrains me. Straining my neck, I see something glinting on the ground.

"I think Lennon hexed him. It's a crystal, it's bleeding black into the natural purple coloring. I think it made it easier to manipulate and amplify Ciaran's natural ambition." Walking to his bag hanging off of one of the horses, he rummages around and pulls out a glass jar with a metal lid. "I'm going to collect it for the council to inspect. Stay here."

>*We're going to hunt, Báirseach. Call if you need us.*< Onyx's voice rumbles, and it reminds me that we need to eat as well.

I'll talk to the men, the shelter is the other side of the lake. Meet us there when you're done? Giving a regal nod to my words, the dragons take flight.

Turning back, I notice Egan and Murphy are already pulling out some jerky and fruit. Cathmor is carefully scooping the crystal off the ground. After putting the lid on, he lays his hand on Ciaran's forehead.

"He's out cold. We may need to sling him over a horse for the way home if he doesn't wake soon." He gently moves Ciaran's limbs, so he's in a more comfortable position but leaves him where he is.

While we sit on the ground eating a light supper, we discuss Lennon, the crystal, and the residual effects that Ciaran might suffer.

Edan is literally playing in the fire. Casey and Mori are on the side of the road, Mori making mud and Casey planting daisies.

"Who knows how long Ciaran's been carrying that crystal. I doubt he suspected his uncle of bespelling him." Egan tosses his apple core to his horse then picks up the jar. Bringing it close to his face, he studies the damaged crystal. "Why did it turn black?"

"I've read about this. It's dark magic manipulating someone's mind." Murphy leans forward dangling his hands over his bent knees. "He must have been using up the limited power of the crystal. The blackness is the expended power."

"I've heard that, too, though I've never actually seen it before." Cathmor leans back on his palms, stretching his legs out and resting them against my thigh. "I fear with as much power as Lennon was using, he may have turned Ciaran's mind."

This saddens me. Ciaran wasn't the best of boyfriends, but if some of his early behavior was driven by Lennon, well . . . it's almost understandable. What he's done, though. How cruel he became? Deep down, that must have been who he was, just amplified by the crystal. Shaking my head, I decide to let the council deal with him. I have other more pressing matters to deal with.

"Can one of you check on Ciaran while I pack up? I asked Onyx and Liam to meet us at the camp. It's just a bit further, then we can relax for the night." Dusting my hands against my thighs, I make a small flame in my hand and burn the trash from our dinner.

※

We travel by horseback for another hour, and as we take a bend in the road towards the lake, we stop short. Five men are on the road, hands outstretched.

Unsheathing our swords, we dismount and get off the road, approaching slowly. Edan, Casey, and Mori hover above us, steam puffing out of their snouts. We use the trees as cover, and we get a better view when we're a few yards away.

Their hair color varies, but the style does not. Each has the sides of their heads shaved, the remaining hair tied back with multiple bands and falling to their waists.

Their blue trousers are tucked into leather boots that reach their knees. They have shirts similar to ours but with a stiff, thin band at the neck. Slung like a cloak across their backs, are animal hides.

One man notices us and starts shouting in a language I don't know. I look across to Cathmor. "Do you know what he's saying? Do you know who they are?"

I'm startled, but I don't panic. It appears they're stuck on the other side of the barrier.

"Pirates. We've been invaded. I know some of the words. . . . I think the barrier is still there. They can't go any further. Can you see it?" Laying a hand on my thigh, Cathmor keeps me from edging too close.

"I see a shimmer. It must be. They look like they're feeling something solid." Attempting to steady my breathing, I place a hand on my stomach. "What should we do?"

"We keep the dragons away until we know how many of them there are. Draw your swords." Cathmor delivers that command to all of us, and I get a glimpse of the part of him that is an Enforcer.

The men must do some communication with their dragon counterparts, because the dragonlings zip into cloak pockets.

"Wait. Let me have Onyx fly over. If he stays high enough he might be able to tell us how many men there are."

Cathmor sends me a grin. "Aye, Báirseach. Good plan."

Onyx? I scan the sky as I call out.

>*Báirseach?*<

Can you fly over the lake? There are invaders present. We need to know how many we are dealing with.

>*As you command.*<

Anxiously we wait, the horses sidestepping as they feed off of our nervousness. Maybe it's just *my* nerves. The men almost seem bored as they sit relaxed on their mounts.

Glancing down the road, I notice that there are now only three men, quietly and furiously arguing with each other. Finally, one of the men, younger and shorter than the others, cautiously steps forward.

"You magicked this ice wall?" His speech is halting and heavily accented.

"No. Another Warlock did that. But you can't pass it without magic!" Cathmor yells back.

A look of alarm crosses the invader's face, and he points to us as he speaks to his peers. Similar looks cross their faces, and another man peels off to retreat. Shouts of excitement rise next as Onyx flies over and lands behind us.

>*There is one here, the second seems to be following the other man back to camp and seven around the fire. I know not if any were inside.*< Onyx pads forward and sits beside me.

The invader yells across, seemingly astonished at how close the dragon is to me. "Is your dragon?"

Cathmor starts to answer, but I place a hand out, stopping him. "Let me answer."

Dismounting, I hand my reins to Egan. Speaking to all my men, I disclose, "Onyx saw ten men. He does not know if there are others inside the shelter. I'm going to go talk to that man. I'll stay on this side of the ward."

I start walking and smile when I hear the jingle of the tackle as my men follow behind me. Onyx, too, strides forward in surprisingly light hops. Hovering behind us, I can feel Liam and Flynn.

As we approach, the invader's eyes grow larger, his words stuttering out, "Dr-dr-agons! Th-the Dr-dragons!"

32

At the sight of the dragons, the invader pales, his eyes roll back, and he slumps into a faint.

"Now's a good time to practice your earth powers, Daisy. Focus on a vine, imagine it stretching and binding his hands. With your hands, pretend you are pulling rope. Remember will and intent." Cathmor tilts his head to the plants on the side of the road.

I raise a hand, and a lone vine lifts up. I pull my hand towards me, and the vine slithers forward. Casey flies to my shoulder, and I feel a boost of power.

I miss the man's hands on my first pass, so we cross the barrier to get closer. Then I almost bind Cathmor's hands as well where he's holding the invader's hands together. But my third try is successful.

"Close the spell, Daisy." Giving me space, Cathmor continues to instruct me.

"Bind and stay. So mote it be." As soon as I'm done, the bindings tighten.

"What's the plan, Cathmor?" Murphy stands guarding the road, sword drawn.

"We take our prisoner to his friends and try to get them to come willingly to Lámhach and face the council."

No sooner has Cathmor finished his sentence than men come running from the far side of the lake. They are brandishing swords and metal-tipped spears.

I don't know if it's the security of being with my men or the bond with the dragons, but I feel confident and unhurried. Whatever happens next, we will be fine.

Egan passes me his sword, and with a flick of his wrists has two large balls of fire floating above the palms of his hands. He lobs them in a continuous motion in the path of the men.

Murphy is making a cupping motion, and waves start breaking over the edge of the lake, growing bigger with each pass. One wave catches a man, drawing him into the lake.

Cathmor raises his arms then slowly draws them together until the palms meet. The trees creak as they bend towards the road. Vines are slithering along the road, tripping and binding the men's legs.

Onyx roars behind me, grabbing a man, flying high before dropping him.

"No! Stop! Don't kill them!" I stay behind my men, screaming.

>*As you command, Báirseach*.< Onyx drops back and lands with a thud behind me.

Egan and Murphy pull their powers back, and it's only then that I see their dragon bondmates sitting on their shoulders. Casey is on all fours, back arched, claws dug into Cathmor's muscles as my mate continues to bind each man.

I hunch forward, hands braced on my knees and fight the nausea bubbling in my gut. I think I'm hyperventilating. Two men were just killed in front of me. Black spots float in front of my eyes, and I slowly kneel on the ground, breathing deeply.

"*Mo Chroí*." Egan rubs circles on my back then speaks to Murphy and Cathmor. "I'm taking her to the shelter. The dragons can guard her. Hopefully, our wagon is still useable and we can use it to move the men."

Murphy lifts me in his arms giving me a hard kiss on the lips. "I'll see you soon, Love."

Egan has mounted a horse, and Murphy gently passes me up to

him. Cathmor steps up before we can leave. Gripping my face, he pulls me forward for a soft kiss.

"You did well stopping us, Daisy. We'll talk more at the shelter." Loping off, he checks on Ciaran, then approaches the bound men.

They are yelling in their language, wriggling away as Murphy and Cathmor disarm them. When they all fall silent, I peer around Egan to find that Liam and Flynn are sitting on their haunches, staring at the prisoners.

With a small laugh, I straighten, releasing a shaky laugh. "I have no problem fighting trolls or dealing with pixies. I've even grown used to the dragons, though now it's easier, as they feel like they are part of me." I hug Egan's arm to me, and he accommodates me by wrapping it around my torso. "But I've never seen a real fight. I've never seen a man die of anything other than natural causes."

"We are taught *how* to fight. How to defend ourselves." Egan sighs, "But I've never fought before. All I could think of was keeping you safe. I might have killed them all, Sage, to protect you."

Twisting, I reach back and press a kiss on Egan's jaw. "Thank you. But I don't want that for you. Not for any of you. I love you, Egan."

"I love you, Sage."

***

Egan leaves me at the firepit to start a fire with Edan, while he makes sure the shelter is clear. He comes out, dragging some fur-covered bags and throws them into the back of the cart. I feed the fire, pulling my cloak close.

Night is falling by the time Egan gets the horse hitched to the wagon. Onyx, who is circling overhead, lands by the fire, stretching out long and resting his massive head on his claws.

Moving closer to Onyx I lean on his side, waiting for my men, and trying to decide where we go from here. There's still the barrier at the Midding Gate. It drove Onyx and the other dragons to the stables, despite having bonds. That means that even though I have magic through my bonds with my mates, I may not be able to pass the gate.

There's also the matter of the pirates. Were they driven to go through the Midding Gate because they, too, are powerless? If so, are they stuck living with us?

My head is pounding by the time I hear the cart on the road. Rising, I wait for it to stop in the yard. Ciaran is awake, but even in the dim light I can tell that he is shaky and pale. His eyes skip all over, from me to the dragons, over the prisoners, and starting all over again.

"What's happening? Where's my uncle? Why are my hands bound? Sage, honey, where are we?" Ciaran sounds like a lost child, and my heart clenches.

With a gentle empathetic voice, Murphy responds, "Ciaran, I'm going to take you inside. Sage will follow soon, and then we'll talk."

The prisoners are all sitting silently in the back of the cart. Probably due to Flynn and Liam following close behind. Cathmor reaches in and motions for the one who was conversing with us to come forward.

He helps the bound man to the ground and leads him to the fire. As soon as the pirate is seated, Cathmor squats beside him.

"What is your name? Why are you here?"

"Name is Bjorn. We want dragon. Very rare. Much coin for scale, horn, claw." The man keeps his focus on Cathmor, avoiding any eye contact with the dragons present.

Casey flies out of Cathmor's pocket, whips the man on the nose with her little tail, and then comes to sit on my lap.

"Is baby dragon?"

Taking the daisy that Casey conjures for me, I answer, "No, she's very special." Sticking the daisy in my hair, I huff. "I can't allow you to hunt the dragons."

"They are not . . . enemy?" Bjorn seems to be hunting through his limited vocabulary.

"No. They're our friends and help us when needed." I feel the need to stress again, "You can't have *any* of the dragons."

Frowning, the man pulls out a book from his pocket. Running a finger down a page he stops, reads then looks up. "We have a pact with Báirseach. Long time. We come to get our due. We leave . . ." Again Bjorn flips through his book, searching. "We leave weapons. Is pact."

Jumping up, I speak as firmly as I can, "Your pact is out of date.

You need to speak with the council. We have no need for your weapons, and I cannot allow you to harm the dragons."

Shaking his head fiercely, Bjorn returns to his native language, pounding his bound fists into his thigh in frustration. The other prisoners start speaking, too, and it's obvious Bjorn is telling them what I've said.

This continues on for a time until finally the day crashes in on me. "Enough! Nothing will get decided tonight. We need to talk to the council and debate all this. Right now, we are going to all get settled for the night. Tomorrow, we leave for Lámhach."

33

Dragging my feet, I make my way to the shelter. Cathmor and Egan stay in the yard to get the prisoners settled, the dragons agreeing to keep watch over them. I don't want to be outside and deal with the men I can hardly communicate with. Men that the Báirseach before me made some kind of pact with that hurt my dragons. I know it needs to be dealt with, but it's not something I can do on my own.

Staring at the wood door, I hesitate. Once I step inside, I'll have to face Ciaran. My left eye twitches at the conversation to come. He appears to not know what's going on. But can I trust that? His behavior in the days leading up to Samhain and all the weeks that followed, can it be blamed on a spell cast by Lennon?

The latch releases easily when I push down, and I untie my cloak as I enter. Murphy is sitting with a mug at the rough table, Mori has a drop of tea formed in his paws and is sipping at it. I glance around, but Ciaran is nowhere to be found. Laying my cloak over the chair across from Murphy, I place both hands atop it and support my weight.

"Where's Ciaran?"

Murphy spins the mug, takes a sip, then looks up at me. With a deep sigh, he replies, "I had him go lay down. He's . . . not well."

Pulling the chair out, I flop down and lay my arms across the table, my fingertips brushing Murphy's hands. "Does he remember anything?"

"He was angry I was keeping him bound. He ranted and raved that it was all Lennon's fault, and then . . ." Murphy snaps his fingers, "He went blank for a second. Then he looked at me confused and muttering. I think without the crystal's influence, his mind is fighting to find its way back. It's sad to see him like that."

Murphy lays a hand over mine, rising and pulling me up with him. "Come lay down. It's probably best if we get some rest, and tomorrow . . . tomorrow, we bring the council in. We have quite a story to tell them."

Laying my head on Murphy's arm as he guides us to a bedroom, I relate what little I've learned about the pact made between the invaders and the last Báirseach.

"That's troubling. I know you're worried and overwhelmed, Love. But Egan, Cathmor, and I will be there by your side. As will the dragons. I'm sure with the council's help, we can come to a resolution." Pressing me to sit on the bed, he kneels before me and unlaces my boots. I'm too tired to object or try to do it myself. "Rest, Love. As my mam says, 'Everything will look better in the morning.'"

The sound of murmured conversation wakes me in the morning. Flipping to my back, I'm aware that I'm the only one in the bed, the spot where Murphy had been sleeping is cold.

Tossing back the covers, I search for my shoes with my toes, grimacing at putting day-old sweaty socks back on. Leaving my boots untied, I shuffle out to the main room to look for my pack for fresh clothes.

Egan and Cathmor have the table set with bread and fruit, mugs of tea wafting fragrant hints of chamomile and honey—enticing me to sit down. Ciaran is slouched sullenly with a mug in his hand, staring at Cathmor.

Egan brightens when he spies me shuffling to the table, "Morning, *Mo Chroí*. Did you sleep well?"

Yawning, I cover my mouth and mutter. "Good morning, Egan. Morning Cathmor, Ciaran." I take a seat between my two bondmates and reach for a mug of tea. "Where's Murphy?"

"He's helping prepare the wagon. We'd like you to ask the dragons to fly us back. If we can ride and they can carry the wagon, we should return by lunch." Cathmor puts an arm along the back of my chair and kisses the top of my head.

"How's she going to talk to the dragons?" Ciaran scoffs. "Or is this something you've been hiding from me? The ability to speak to dragons?"

Sighing, I rip apart a piece of bread, before answering. "I'm not sure what you know, or remember Ciaran. And frankly, at this point, everything you say is suspect. But a lot has happened in the last month. You'll have to wait to hear about it when I give a report to the council." With a knife I slice a strawberry and fold it into my bread. "I *can* speak to the dragons. That's all you need to know for now."

This does not sit well with Ciaran, but he turns his attitude on Cathmor. "When will you release my wrists, Enforcer?"

Cathmor angrily eyes the other man over his mug, "That's for the council to decide." He raises an eyebrow when Ciaran starts to object. "No arguments, there are many things I am arresting you for. And make no mistake, you are under arrest. The main item, though, is kidnapping and attempted murder." Slamming his mug to the table, Cathmor stands and starts pacing, fury driving each step as he lets loose on Ciaran. "You almost killed Sage and yourself on the side of that volcano, Ciaran. I don't care if you were under a spell, to me, that is unforgivable."

Ripping his cloak off a hook, Cathmor swings it over his shoulders and storms out, the slam of the door punctuating his words. My hands tremble as I take a bite of my strawberry-filled bread. I forgot how intimidating Cathmor can be. He's always gruff, though lately he's been very sweet to me. But the Cathmor that just slammed out of the house? That's the Enforcer who was so condescending on Samhain.

Egan gives me a side hug, whispering in my ear, "Why don't I take

Ciaran outside and leave you to freshen up? Then you can speak to the dragons, and we can be on our way. All will be well, *Mo Chroí*. All will be well."

I nod against his chest, flicking my gaze to Ciaran. He's staring at his bound wrists in confusion, brow furrowed. He doesn't resist when Egan instructs him to stand and follows my mate meekly outside.

The tension drains from my body when the door clicks shut. I flex my hands around my mug and quickly finish breaking my fast. My pack is leaning against the hearth, and I take it back to my room to change, bracing myself against all that is to come.

I have always been more comfortable on the fringes of society, but Ciaran, my bondings, and the dragons have dragged me right into the center of the unknown. I need to be strong. If I could live and thrive for twenty-seven years as a Mundane, I can adapt to my new world. I have to.

34

The dragons agree to carry everyone back to Lámhach. Cathmor says he'll ask for some of the champions to return for the horses. Onyx is joking — *I think* — about accidentally dropping the wagon halfway on top of a mountain. The pirates stare wide-eyed at the thick vines running underneath the wagon, some struggling to climb out when it's revealed *how* we will be traveling. One snap of Flynn's jaws settles them down.

I will ride on Onyx, along with half of the supplies. There's an argument between Liam and Flynn, which results in dirt and snow showering us as they stomp and circle each other. Neither dragon wants to carry Ciaran.

Stop! One of you needs to step up and carry him. Along with Egan and Murphy. My words halt the dragons, and they stand proud, huffing in anger.

Flynn lets out a loud roar and a thin stream of fire, before stomping over to the men. >*I shall take them, Báirseach. It will be an honor to carry your bondmates. And the scum, if I must.*<

Liam slinks to Cathmor, head hanging. >*I'm sorry, Báirseach. That was unbecoming of me.*<

Laughter fills me at the ridiculous dragon. His body language may be saying he feels bad, but his tone is smug. He's not really sorry that Flynn will be carrying Ciaran.

Wiping my eyes, I nod to my mates, "The dragons are ready."

The trip is uneventful, save for the struggle to get Ciaran near and then on the massive red dragon. It's also very quick. The mountains are put behind us, and we are soon soaring above the dragon stables.

In just a month, new homes have been built. I see the champions running to their dragons, familiar and unfamiliar faces running from the houses, as well as Renny and Master Riordan stepping out from the large stone stable.

I instruct the dragons to deposit the wagon in the large pasture that marks the beginning of the dragon lands. It rolls free once it's on the ground, and Onyx and I land heavily before it to stop the momentum.

Flynn and Liam land further out, choosing and *needing* more area due to their larger size. As they stride towards us, the sound of confused voices reaches us before the crowd appears around the stables.

"Sage, what is the meaning of this? How . . . where . . .? Why are there dangerous dragons in our field?" Master Riordan takes command of the situation, stuttering at the sight of Flynn and Liam.

"It's a very long story, Master. One I'd like to only recount once if possible." Walking down Onyx's spine to dismount, I approach. Straightening my ponytail, I gesture for my bondmates to bring Ciaran forward. "We did have a few problems, and we need to speak to the council. Please be assured that the dragons are not dangerous. Flynn is the red, and Liam is the silver." The dragons dip their heads as I introduce them. Looking past Master Riordan, I address Laurel, "Could you or one of the other champions please get Elder Thyme and the council? I'm sure they saw us approach, but we have prisoners, and it is urgent."

"Of course, Sage." Laurel gives one more awestruck glance at the unfamiliar dragons before spinning and running towards the village.

As I move to speak with Master Riordan again, my eye catches the four black dragons who had stayed behind in Lámhach. Each is gazing at me and striding forward. Their girth makes the people shy away, and they take advantage to sit in a line to my left.

>*Báirseach*< They greet me and bow their heads.

With a wide grin, I run to them, gently rubbing a hand over a snout, or leg of each. *Hello, my dragons. I have missed you. But tell me, how did the invaders get past you? We found them by the Lake of Sorrows.*

>*We were not here. We were training with young Renny out in the dragon lands. We've just returned and were told what happened . . . there are no excuses. We failed you.*< Raven, Laurel's dragon admits what had occurred.

Never. You did not fail me. You could not have known. Rest easy. They each relax, spreading out and laying in the sun at my words.

Turning back, I smile as I walk to Master Riodran. Murphy is there as well, Renny clinging to his side. "Hi, Renny!"

"Hey, Sage. I missed you." he squeaks when Murphy ruffles his shaggy brown hair. "Stop. I might have missed you, too, Murphy."

"Did you learn something new while I was gone?" I cross my arms and question the intern.

Renny bounces on his toes, eyes sparkling and his words rushing out. "I did! The champions let me observe their training, and they taught me how to care for them and, Sage! Sage! Ronan let me ride Slate!"

Pleased, I praise him, "Great job, you and I will talk later. Perhaps you learned something I don't know. I'm eager to find out."

Master Riordan eyes the dragons before asking me. "What of the eggs and hatchlings, Sage? Did they make it? Did you leave them at the lava pools?"

Taking a deep breath, I admit, "The eggs . . . there was a complication. But it is all part of our story and must wait for the council. I'm sorry, but I think . . . I think it must be relayed in order for it all to be clear."

"I'll be patient, Sage. I trust your judgment." Master Riordan claps his hands and address the spectators, "Back to your homes! This is a council matter now."

As they disperse, I notice one woman hanging back. She has long black hair and is thin as a twig. Arms crossed, she warily eyes the dragons before calling out. "Egan!"

My bondmate glances up at his name, then smiles as he lopes forward. "Jasmine. Sage, come meet my cousin."

Excusing myself, I leave Murphy talking with Master Riordan and Renny, jogging to Egan's side.

Placing his arm around my shoulders, Egan introduces us. "Sage, this is my cousin Jasmine. Jasmine, this is Sage, my bondmate."

With a scowl, Jasmine eyes me from tip to toe. "Aye, I heard about that. Sage. You are the reason I was pulled across the Midding Gate?"

"I . . . yes, it is because of me, that you are stuck here." I accept that though Ciaran cast the spell, it was his obsession with me that drove him to it. "I apologize for disrupting your life in such a manner."

Jasmine purses her lips, giving me a hard glare. Then suddenly, she starts laughing. "I can't keep it up. Oh, Sage, it's grand to meet you. I know this is supposed to be a bad thing, but living here? I feel like I belong. Everyone has been very welcoming. They built us a house, and your parents are thinking of moving their store here so that I can help them, and they can be closer to you." Tears leak from the corners of her eyes. "For the first time in my life, I'm with others like me. And the dragons! The sight of the dragons alone, has made it wonderful." She steps forward to hug me. "Don't let an ex-boyfriend's mistakes get to you. You have nothing to be sorry for. He chose his actions. You are a victim of that just like I am. Don't ever apologize for someone else's mistakes."

I didn't realize I needed to hear that until just now. With a warm feeling in my chest, I lean in for another hug, "Thank you, Jasmine. Welcome to Lámhach."

༄

My parents arrive with the council, and I run into their arms. "Mam. Da. I missed you both so much."

Mam brushes my bangs to the side as she scans my face. "Dear heart, what's happened? It's only been a month. We weren't expecting you until the vernal equinox. Did the invaders catch up with you?"

"We've had quite a time. There's so much to tell you. But I need to tell you, I have a third bondmate." Turning my head, I smile sheepishly at Da. "It's Cathmor."

Da can't hide his pleasure and looking over my head he yells out, "Oy, Padraig. Your son bonded my Sage!"

Padriag bounds over, and lifts me in a hug. With a laugh, I cling to his shoulders and gaze down at a shorter, greyer version of my mate.

"Da! Are you trying to steal my Daisy?" Cathmor pulls me from his da's arms and nestles me in front of him, my back flush with his chest.

Before our parents can get too carried away in conversation — did my mom say grandchildren? — Elder Thyme gains everyones' attention.

"I know we are all excited to see our loved ones, but let's have some order. Master Riordan has provided the main room of the stable to meet. The champions, save for Cathmor, will guard the prisoners. The dragons, I trust, are safe in the field, Sage?"

"Yes, they are safe for the villagers to approach if any are brave enough to try. Perhaps, Renny could be in charge of that?" I rush to assure her that my dragons pose no threat.

Raising her eyebrows, Elder Thyme comments, "Indeed."

The three council members enter the space first, taking seats on hay bales. My bondmates follow, with Ciaran in tow. I enter asking, "May our parents be present as well?" Murphy's parents arrived at some point, and I wasn't sure if all would be welcome at the meeting.

"We'll call them if we feel there is something they need to be informed about. For now, I think we should keep the meeting small. Master Riordan, if you could let them know we will call them as needed?" Elder Quinn answers my question and sends Master Riordan to speak to our parents.

Once we are all seated and Master Riordan has returned, Elder Thyme takes control of the meeting. "Now then, Sage. Start at the beginning."

35

Relating the journey was a series of stops and starts. When I told them Onyx followed us, Elder Quinn questioned Cathmor about the dragon's behavior. When we explained waking up to Cathmor's arrival and Ciaran's desertion, there were numerous comments and inquiries—all to the point and with the council keeping neutral expressions.

We got stuck on that topic for awhile as the elders attempted to interrogate Ciaran and were exposed to his ranting and confusion. Elder Thyme finally silenced him with a spell before asking, "What is wrong with Ciaran?"

Cathmor dug in his pocket for the crystal and passed the jar to the council. "We believe Lennon was controlling his nephew. This needs to be studied, but he's been acting erratically since it fell off of him on the way home."

"Lennon?" Elder Quinn inspects the crystal then passes the jar on. "Was Lennon with you?"

Murphy picked up the story, explaining our theory that Lennon aided Ciaran. He described the ice barrier and how it differed from the ward on the Midding Gate.

I broke in at this point. "Is the ward still up?"

"It is, we were hoping to get some resolution when you returned." Elder Thyme pauses and spares a glance for Ciaran. "I'm not sure what help he will be if he remains ... confused."

Determined to see if I can pass through with my bondmates, I move and discuss finding Ciaran's horse, the book, and the trolls.

This grabs the Elders' interest, and for the first time, I see concern cross their faces. "What book is this?" Elder Roarke asks.

Egan reaches into his pack and passes over the book *The Power of the Elements* and the note we'd found in Ciaran's things. Passing from elder to elder, the play of emotions across their faces is interesting. Elder Roarke is amused by the book, Elder Quinn is angry, but Elder Thyme? Elder Thyme is furious. Her fury grows when she reads Ciaran's notes.

"He wanted to find the elemental dragons? He knew enough to try to bind you to find them?" I have never seen Elder Thyme as anything but calm and reserved — until right now, as she shakes the paper in Ciaran's face. "What were you trying to do? Do you know what his plan was?" The last question she asks of Cathmor.

"He spoke of taking over the council and the academy. He will not get the elementals," Cathmor asserts firmly. I look to my men, knowing the dragons are tucked in their cloaks. Each slightly shakes their heads. I take that to mean now is not the time to expose them.

"Of course not. That would be dangerous." Setting the note and book to the side with the crystal, Elder Thyme composes herself, folding her hands into her lap. "Let us continue."

Murphy picks up our tale, though he's stopped when he describes my kidnapping. At that point, I had to relate the five days with Lennon and Ciaran and how they grew more and more delusional. I spoke of the trek to the volcano, Lennon's collapse, and Ciaran's and my close call on the side of the path.

Elder Thyme cuts in, "Were they the elemental dragon eggs?"

With a sigh, I lean into Egan's shoulder. At this rate we were never getting through the whole story. "No. Instead we almost died. Cathmor sent out vines, he almost got us to safety. It's when our binding happened."

"What do you mean he *almost* got you to safety?"

"You have a third binding?"

"How did you get off the volcano?"

The questions ring out one on top of the other. What do I answer first?

Cathmor reaches over Egan and grips my arm. Pushing up my sleeve, he lifts my ivy mark for inspection. "Aye. Bonded and mated. We are all bonded and mated with Sage." Kissing my wrist, he releases it and gives me a wink. "It is a lucky thing she completed the bonding when she did. The second it happened, my vines burned away, and I fell back. Flynn, the red dragon, swooped in and picked Sage and Ciaran off the volcano."

Silence rings. It stretches on. Elder Thyme is staring at me, several times opening her mouth but closing it again without saying anything.

Master Riordan finally breaks the silence. "Did the eggs hatch? Were there any problems?"

Elder Thyme overrides him, waving a hand. "We'll get to the dragons in a minute. Tell me about the prisoners you brought back. They landed a day and a half ago and didn't stop until they got through the Midding Gate. The spell compelled them. Master Riordan relayed that they stopped briefly before heading for the pass. They knew where they were going."

"They did know. Only one of them was able to communicate with us. When we encountered them they were stopped by the ice barrier. We managed to corral and bind them at the Lake of Sorrows." Sitting forward, I let my hands dangle between my knees, looking earnestly at the council. "He was able to tell us that they had a pact with the Báirseach. They supplied weapons and were given permission to take a dragon."

"We will not recognize that pact. They must not be allowed to take any dragon. There is no leeway we will give there."

Liam speaks to me, startling me and almost making me fall to the floor of the stable. Murphy catches me as I turn my concentration inward. *>You could make a new pact with them and the council. Think, Báirseach. We can supply what they want. Dragons lose scales and claws all the time. And horns? Even we die.<*

"Sage! Miss Sage!" Elder Thyme's strident voice grabs my attention, and I look her way as I settle myself against Murphy. "What has come over you, girl?"

"I was thinking. At the moment, the invaders are stuck here. They can't cross the barrier to the north, nor can they cross the Midding Gate. If we manage to take the ward down, we can still rework the pact." Feeling more confident, I continue. "We can send Witches to the dragon lands to collect scales and claws that have been shed by the dragons. Occasionally, offer a pair of horns if they come across the corpse of a dragon."

"I need to walk and think. Come, we can continue this in the yard." Elder Thyme leads the way past the forge and the half wall, the Midding Gate visible in front of us.

Shaking her head, Elder Thyme rejects my suggestion. "We cannot speak for the dragons. The Báirseach was . . . he was misguided and drunk on power. That cannot happen again."

"We can try to speak to Bjorn. He's the invader we were communicating with at the lake." Walking in front of the council, I continue. "We can try. Otherwise, they will keep coming."

"You don't know what you're asking. In order to make a new pact, we need a new Báirseach. We, the council, will not allow that to happen." Elder Thyme raises a hand when I move to argue.

"Stick to your dragons, Sage. We'll deal with the invaders and the pact."

"You need me." Angry now, I speak over the end of her words. "I will take care of my dragons. No one, will take them from me." Just as with the bindings, the words come without thought, without me able to stem their flow.

"What do you mean *your* dragons?" Elder Thyme looks at me suspiciously.

Raising a hand behind me, I wiggle my fingers. *Come,* I call to the dragons I can sense nearby. Addressing the council again, I state passionately, "They are *all my* dragons." Edan, Casey, and Mori land on my outstretched arm, while thud after thud resounds as Liam, Flynn, Onyx, the black dragons, and many others begin to land behind me.

Dimly I'm aware of the few villagers exclaiming as they arrive. The council stares at the dragons then switch their focus to me.

"Sage?" I don't know who speaks. But I give the words the Goddess compels me to speak.

"I am Báirseach."

Acknowledgments

Thank you for reading. This book would not have been possible without the encouragement and support of my family. My boys were occasionally called on for research, and they stepped up. My love, my husband, for listening to me talk about plots, characters, and magic . . . just as a sounding board until I figured it out myself.

Mercedes, my friend, my muse . . . you really kept me going. Checking in daily. Giving me sneak peeks of your own work. I can never thank you enough.

To my alphas, you kept me going with your love of my story and Onyx — the best dragon ever. You guys definitely gave me awesome ideas when I would get stuck. Rachel, Sue, Christina, Sarah Ann, and Sarah M., you rock! I appreciate every comment and feedback you offered.

To my betas, Sandi, and Kelly — thank you for all your hard work and checking the final product. I know it was a quick turn around, but you guys did it. This book would not have been done in time without you.

Thank you Jo for the beautiful cover, CA for the original artwork, and Michelle for the wonderful editing job.

And last but not least, to the entire Indie author community. So many words of wisdom, advice, and encouragement shared.

Thank you from the bottom of my heart.

About The Author

VB Gilbert is a Texas native, a wife, mom, and lover of books and coffee.

Reading has always kept her sane. Being able to disappear into a story has long been a stress reliever for her. When she is not writing or reading, she is attending school functions, watching Marvel movies, and geeking out on *Buffy*, *Firefly*, *Doctor Who*, and, of course, *Hitchhiker's Guide to the Galaxy*.

Follow on Facebook for early teasers and up to date news about releases
Or just to have fun
https://www.facebook.com/groups/VGBookLovers/
Follow me for teasers, character pics, and just fun pics that inspire me
https://instagram.com/veronicagilbertauthor
Twitter
https://twitter.com/author_vb
BookBub
https://www.bookbub.com/authors/vb-gilbert
Goodreads
https://www.goodreads.com/author/show/19154682.VB_Gilbert

VB GILBERT

REDS OF SUMMER

THRIVE SERIES BOOK ONE

VB GILBERT

BLUES OF WINTER

THRIVE SERIES BOOK TWO

VB GILBERT

HUNTERS OF SPRING

THRIVE SERIES BOOK THREE

OTHER BOOKS BY VB GILBERT

Thrive Series
Reds of Summer
Blues of Winter
Hunters of Spring - Winter 2019

Women of Bohemia
Savannah Smiles - TBD

Printed in Great Britain
by Amazon